"Here's To You, Libby, Darlin'. Now That You Know Who I Really Am, What Do You Intend To Do About It?"

He didn't have a clue how she'd found out, but it had been bound to happen from the second he'd introduced himself to her as an architect. What kind of fool was he, thinking he'd find "regular love" wearing a disguise?

He really couldn't blame Libby one bit for being so angry, as would he if it had happened in reverse. But it wasn't the worst lie that had ever been told. Hell. What if he'd actually been an architect who tried to pass himself off as David Halstrom? Surely that would have been a larger crime and would have angered her even more.

He drained his glass, refilled it, then sat on a leather couch, staring south, wondering what to do next. For the first time in his life, David didn't have a clue.

Dear Reader,

What fun it was to work on this series with three great pals who are also terrific writers—Joan Hohl, Leslie LaFoy and Kasey Michaels. In the planning stage, we really kept the Internet buzzing with our back-and-forth e-mails.

Here's hoping we've managed to bring you four terrific stories about people who all deserve to win a million dollars.

Happy reading!

Best wishes,

Mary McBride

MARY McBRIDE

THE MAGNATE'S TAKEOVER

Published by Silhouette Books
America's Publisher of Contemporary Romance

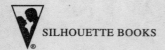 SILHOUETTE BOOKS
®

ISBN-13: 978-0-373-76904-9
ISBN-10:   0-373-76904-0

THE MAGNATE'S TAKEOVER

Visit Silhouette Books at www.eHarlequin.com

Printed in U.S.A.

MARY McBRIDE

When it comes to writing romance, historical or contemporary, Mary McBride is a natural. What else would anyone expect from someone whose parents met on a blind date on Valentine's Day, and who met her own husband—whose middle name happens to be Valentine!—on February 14th, as well?

She lives in Saint Louis, Missouri, with her husband and two sons. Mary loves to hear from readers. You can write to her c/o P.O. Box 411202, Saint Louis, MO 63141, or contact her online at McBride101@aol.com.

Prologue

Well, my darlings, it's almost Halloween and I have oodles of treats and goodies for you. Shall we talk about the RB again? That oh-so-generous and oh-so-mysterious Reclusive Billionaire is believed to have struck again, anointing a candidate somewhere in the Midwest—that would be Fly-Over Country for most of you, my dear readers—with his largesse.

Alas, our information does not extend beyond mere geography at this date. Surely someone out there in the vast Heartland has a clue that he or she would be more than delighted to share. Call me, darling. I am, as they say, all ears.

Sam Balfour slapped the newspaper on the desktop as if he were swatting a fly. "This woman is worse than a rabid bloodhound," he said.

S. Edward Balfour IV, otherwise known as Uncle Ned, glanced up from his own newspaper. "She's persistent, I'll grant you that. We could use a few more like her on our team."

"Our team, as you so casually put it, Uncle Ned, is about to be exposed by this harpy. Doesn't that worry you in the least?"

"No," his uncle said. "Actually, I have other things to worry about. Here." He handed a large book across the desk. "Take a look at this. Tell me what you think."

Sam, still grinding his teeth, flipped through the pages, mostly photographs of old derelict motels in the Midwest. "They're nice pictures," he said, "if you like things like that."

"I do," his uncle said as he reached into his desk drawer to produce a green folder which he passed to Sam. "Take care of this for me, will you?"

"You're crazy, you know, to continue with this little game," Sam cautioned him.

His uncle merely smiled. "I suspect we're all a bit crazy, one way or another. Read through the folder, Sam. Then see that the usual check reaches Miss Libby Jost no later than Friday."

Sam could only sigh. Here we go again...

One

"Here's to you, you magnificent building."

Libby Jost stared out the window and raised her wine glass once again to toast the nearly completed 20-story convention hotel on the other side of the highway just west of St. Louis. Now that it was autumn and the trees were nearly bare, and even across six lanes of traffic, the bright lights of the Halstrom Marquis flickered like rubies in what was left of her red Chianti.

"And here's to you, Mr. Halstrom, whoever you are and if you really do exist. Welcome to the neighborhood." She swallowed the last of the wine, and then a silly, not-too-sober smile played at the edges of her mouth. "What took you so long?"

She put down her empty glass, stood up and then immediately realized she had celebrated a bit too much. Way too much, in fact, for a person who rarely drank at all. Her last drink, incidentally, had been an obligatory glass of champagne on New Year's Eve. She was definitely out of practice, she decided, and figured it was time for a very sobering slap of cold October air, so she flipped the main switch for the outside lights and wobbled out the door.

Once outside, Libby glanced up at the ancient neon No Vacancy sign flickering above the office door. How sad was that? she thought. After all these years, all these decades, it was probably some sort of miracle that the *V,* two *c*'s and half of the *y* still managed to faintly sputter. The mere sight of the sign might have completely depressed her a few months ago, but it didn't tonight. It didn't bother her at all because she knew there would be a brand-new, far better sign very soon, and instead of perpetual vacancies, the old Haven View Motor Court would once more be full of guests and good times.

Again, as she'd done a thousand times these past few weeks, she gave silent thanks to the anonymous Santa Claus who'd sent her a check for fifty thousand dollars in appreciation of her recent book of photographs of old, downtrodden motels in the Midwest. Libby Jost was, first and foremost, a serious photographer who had worked for the St. Louis newspaper for nearly a decade. She'd garnered numerous awards in the past, but most of them came in the form of plaques or framed certificates usually accompanied by long, boring speeches and polite applause. She'd gotten a check for two hundred bucks once for a photo of the Gateway Arch in morning mist, but never anything close to fifty thousand dollars.

The huge, unexpected check not only sustained her pride in her work, but it also provided her the wherewithal to help her aunt Elizabeth, the woman who had raised her here at this run-down motel after the death of her parents in a car accident when Libby was just a toddler.

Aunt Elizabeth hadn't asked for her help, but then she didn't have to. As soon as Libby realized that the fifty-thousand-dollar gift wasn't a joke or a stunt of some kind, but was indeed good as gold according to her bank, she arranged for a leave of absence from the newspaper and began making plans to revive the derelict motel. It was her aunt's dream, after all, and Libby felt she owed it to her to keep that dream alive as long as she possibly could.

And while she was giving thanks, she directed a few of them to the Halstrom Marquis, which soon would be sending its overflow customers across the highway to the newly remodeled, all spiffed-up, ready-to-go Haven View.

Libby was determined to make it happen. The anonymous Santa had given her the money to set it all in motion. She had taken her time to nail down her plans and to budget the money properly. Now she was ready to begin.

Stepping out onto the pebbled drive that wound through the dilapidated little tourist court, she noticed that one of the lampposts was dark. Damn. If it wasn't one irritation, it was another. Exterior bulbs had gotten so expensive, even at the discount stores, and they seemed to burn out way too frequently these days.

Maybe she could let one light go dark for awhile. Maybe no one would even notice. There weren't any guests here, for heaven's sake. But, after another glance at the magnificently illuminated hotel across the highway, Libby sighed. Got to keep up with the Joneses now, she thought, or with the Halstroms as is in this case. She went back into the office in search of a ladder and a light bulb.

Well, this wasn't one of the best ideas she'd ever had, Libby thought ten minutes later as she wobbled and swayed high up on the ladder while trying to juggle a large glass globe, a dead light bulb, a fresh light bulb and the four screws from the lamp. If anything, it was a terrible idea. She could see the paper's headline already: *Woman, inebriated, expires under lamp.*

And if it wasn't a disaster already, it surely became one when a car engine growled behind her, headlights flooding the parking lot and tires biting into the loose gravel of the driveway just behind her. A customer at this time of night? That wasn't at all likely. The motel hadn't had a single customer in three or four weeks.

She tried to look over her shoulder to see who or what it was, but the fierce headlights blinded her. When she heard the car door whip open and then slam shut, her heart leaped into her throat and made it impossible to shout or scream.

This was not good. Not good at all. It was terrible. A strangled little moan broke from her lips.

Then Libby lost her grip and the globe and the light bulbs crashed onto the ground below her, and she was about to crash down, too, on top of all that broken glass when a deep voice said, "Hold still."

Two hands clamped around her waist.

"I've got you," he said. "You're okay. Just relax and let go of the ladder."

Libby, in her total panic, tried to jerk away from his grasp and she held on to the lamppost even tighter than before.

"Dammit," he growled, tightening his grip on her waist. "I said let go. It's okay. I've got you."

He did, indeed, have her.

What else could she do? Libby dragged in a breath, held it and then let go of the lamppost, wondering vaguely if her life was going to flash before her eyes now that it was about to end.

It felt like falling into a giant bear hug. The arms that caught her were warm and encompassing. Then glass crunched under the bear's feet as he turned, took several strides and finally and oh-so-gently set her down.

She was safe, but only for a second. The bear turned on her, his eyes flashing. "What the hell were you doing up there?" he growled. "You could have broken your damn neck."

Libby's heart was pounding like a jackhammer. Her legs felt like jelly, and she was still not exactly sober. Far from it, in fact. But now, instead of feeling tipsy and scared to death, she felt tipsy and mad as hell so she yelled back at the bear, "Well, it's *my* damn neck."

He merely stared at her then, stared hard, as if he were memorizing every feature and angle, every crook and cranny of her body, or else perhaps he was merely calculating the calories there just in case he decided to take a bite out of her.

Belligerently, Libby stared right back, into a face that struck her as more rugged than handsome. Even in the semidarkness of the driveway, she could tell that his eyes were a deep hazel and the line of his chin like granite. He was fairly good-looking, for a bear. She wobbled again, struggling to keep her balance and wound up standing even closer to him. He smelled divine, even though she was too tipsy to identify the scent. Then he smiled. It was a sudden, wonderful surprise of a smile that carved out sexy lines on both sides of his mouth.

"It's a lovely neck," he said, reaching out to touch the hammering pulse in her throat.

Libby blinked. "Thank you," she said. "I think."

Whatever hostility that had flared up so suddenly between them seemed to vanish into the cool night air. She glanced at his car—a dark, sleek Jaguar—and was fairly well convinced that this guy wasn't a thug or a rapist or, for that matter, a paying customer. People who stayed at the Haven View these days tended to drive dirty pickups and dented sedans.

But before she could ask the Jaguar guy just who or what he truly was, he asked her, "Is the boss around?"

Libby almost laughed. Her whole life she'd looked far younger than she actually was. Now, even at age thirty, she could still easily pass for nineteen or twenty. And obviously she didn't look like a "boss," either, in her current panicky and slightly inebriated state.

Well, in reality she wasn't the actual boss here. The Haven View Motor Court belonged to her aunt Elizabeth, after all, as it had for the past fifty years, but while her elderly aunt was in a nursing home recovering from a broken hip, Libby was most definitely in charge.

"The boss," she said, "is currently under the weather, which means I'm temporarily in charge around here." She attempted to stand a bit taller, a bit more steadily, even as her vision seemed to be blurring. Hoping to appear professional in spite of her condition, Libby stuck out her hand. "I'm Libby Jost. What, may I ask, can I do for you?"

His lips curled into another stunning and sexy grin. "I don't think you can do much of anything for anybody at the moment, little Libby." His hand reached out to steady her. "What do you think?"

What did she think? She thought she heard a bit of a Texas twang in his voice, and then she thought she was going to be very, very sick right here in the parking lot if she didn't make it to the office in time.

"Excuse me," she mumbled, then ran as fast as her wobbly legs would allow.

Well, it wasn't the first time he'd encountered a pretty woman who'd had too much to drink, David Halstrom thought, but it was certainly the first time he'd witnessed a woman four feet off the ground clinging to a lamppost or one who looked like an inebriated fallen angel. She was so damn pretty, even in the dim lamplight, with her strawberry blond hair and her spattering of freckles that he'd almost forgotten why he'd come to this derelict hellhole in the first place.

He sighed and supposed he ought to check on her so he walked in the direction of the buzzing, nearly burned-out vacancy sign. He knocked on the door, waited a moment and when nobody answered, he entered what appeared to be the office of this dump which she claimed to manage. Hell. It was already pretty clear to him that she couldn't even manage herself much less a run-down tourist court.

The office was as tawdry as he expected, like something right out of the 1950s if not earlier. It didn't surprise him a bit to see a small black-and-white television with foil-wrapped rabbit ears wedged into a corner of the room, right next to a windowsill lined with half-dead plants. Good God. Did people actually stay here? Did they *pay* to stay here?

There was a floral couch against one wall. On the table in front of it sat a straw-covered bottle of Chianti and an empty glass. The caretaker's poison, no doubt.

He knocked softly on a nearby door, then he opened it a few inches and saw a dimly lit bedroom that wasn't quite as tattered as the lobby. There was a faint odor of lavender in the small room, and in the center of the bed, beneath the covers, he recognized a Libby-sized lump.

Good, he thought. She'd sleep it off and tomorrow she'd have a headache to remind her that cheap wine had its perils.

"Sleep well, angel," he whispered. "When you lose this job, you can come to work for me."

He quietly closed the door and returned to the parking lot.

A quick walk around the dismal property only served to confirm all of David's suspicions. The place was a total wreck in dire need of demolition, which he would be more than happy to arrange. He got back in his car and headed for his hotel on the other side of the highway. As he drove, his thumb punched in his assistant's number on his cell phone.

Jeff Montgomery was probably in the middle of dinner, he thought, but the call wouldn't surprise him nor would David's demand for instant action. The young man had worked for him for five years and seemed to thrive on the stress and the frequent travel as well as the variety of tasks that David tossed his way, from *Make sure my tux is ready by six,* to *Put together a proposal for that acreage in New Mexico.*

This evening David told him, "I need to know everything there is to know about the Haven View Motor Court across from the hotel. Who owns it? Is there any debt? What's the tax situation? Everything. And while you're at it, see what you can dig up on a woman named Libby Jost. Have it on my desk tomorrow morning, Jeff. Ten at the latest."

"You got it, boss" came the instant reply. David Halstrom was used to instant replies.

He was used to getting precisely what he wanted, in fact, and he figured he'd own the ramshackle Haven View Motor Court lock, stock and barrel in a few days, or a week at the very most. And if he didn't exactly own the fallen strawberry-blond angel by then, at least she'd be on his payroll.

Two

At ten o'clock the next morning Libby, in faded jeans and a thick white wool turtleneck, wasn't at all surprised that she had a splitting headache while she followed the painting contractor around Haven View. She couldn't even bear to think about the previous night, even as she wondered what had happened to the handsome bear.

As on most days, a camera hung from a leather strap around her neck because a dedicated photographer never knew when a wonderful picture might present itself. This morning, however, the camera strap felt more like a noose while the camera itself seemed to weigh a lot more than it ever had in the past. She was grateful the contractor didn't walk very fast, which allowed her to sip hot, healing coffee while she tried to interpret his expressions.

Sometimes the man's sandy eyebrows inched together above the bridge of his nose as if he were thinking, *Hmm. This old wood window trim might be a little bit tricky. That won't be cheap.* Other times he narrowed his eyes and bit his lower lip which Libby interpreted as, *There's not enough paint in the state of Missouri to make this crummy place look better.* Once he even sighed rather dramatically and then gazed heavenward, which probably meant he wouldn't take this job no matter how much she offered to pay him.

Finally, the suspense was more than she could stand, not to mention the imagined humiliation when he told her the place wasn't even good enough to paint, so she told the man to take his time, then excused herself. She headed back to the office, pausing once more to look around the foot of the lamppost to make sure she'd picked up every shard of broken glass from last night's sorry incident.

She had almost reached the office door when she heard the familiar growl of a certain sleek automobile. As she turned to watch the dark-green vehicle approach along the gravel driveway, Libby swore she could almost feel the sexual throb of its engine deep in the pit of her stomach. Oh, brother. She wasn't going to drink Chianti again for a long, long time.

Or maybe she was just feeling the deep shame of losing control the way she had the night before. Whoever the guy was and whatever he wanted, his opinion of her must be pretty low. If nothing else, she thought she owed the guy an apology along with a sincere thank-you for rescuing her from all that shattered glass.

She also thought, while staring at his fabulous car, that the vehicle was undoubtedly worth more—way more—than her fifty-thousand-dollar surprise fortune. How depressing was that? Still, it certainly piqued her interest in the man behind the wheel and whatever intentions he might have.

As if by reflex, she put her coffee mug on the ground and lifted her camera, shoving the lens cap in her pocket and glancing to make sure the aperture was set where she wanted it for this relatively bright morning. She snapped him exiting the car.

He seemed taller and more muscular than she remembered from the night before, but that face matched her memory of it perfectly. It was tough. Rugged. Masculine as hell. It was a countenance far better suited to a dusty pickup truck than a shiny luxury sedan.

His face, however, was shielded by his lifted hand as he approached her. Damn. She really wanted to capture those great Marlboro-Man features, especially his wonderful smile lines, but he kept them hidden as he approached.

She lowered the camera. He lowered his hand.

"How are you feeling this morning?" he asked.

Sensing the smirk just beneath his affable grin, Libby quickly forced her lips into a wide, bright smile as she responded, "One hundred percent."

He cocked his head and narrowed his autumn-colored eyes, scrutinizing her face. "Really?"

"Well…" Libby shrugged. The man knew all too well what her condition had been the night before. She had nearly thrown up on him, after all. There wasn't much use denying it. "Maybe ninety-five percent. Actually it's more like eighty-five percent, but definitely trending upward."

"Yeah," he said, bending to pick up her coffee, then placing the mug in her hand. "Booze tends to do that more often than not." Now his gaze strayed from her face, moved down past her turtleneck, paused at her breasts for a second, then focused on her Nikon. "What's the camera for?"

"I'm a photographer." She took a sip from her mug.

"I thought you were a motel sitter."

Libby laughed. "Well, I'm both I guess. I'm Libby Jost." Locals more often than not recognized her name from the photographs in the paper, but it didn't seem to ring even a tiny little bell for Mr. Marlboro Man. She extended her hand. "And you are…?"

"David," he said, reaching out to grip her hand more tightly than she expected. "I'm…" He frowned slightly, then angled his head north in the direction of the hotel across the highway. "I'm the architect of that big shiny box."

At that particular moment the big, shiny, mirrored façade of the Halstrom Marquis was full of lovely blue autumn sky and a few crisp white clouds. Libby loved it more every time she looked at it, she thought.

"It's stunning," she said. "You did a truly spectacular job. And I confess I love taking pictures of it. It's a completely different building from one day to another, even from one minute to another. Today it's like a lovely perpendicular piece of sky."

"Thanks. Just a few more weeks until the grand

opening. Would you like an invitation?" He chuckled rather demonically. "I'm sure the liquor will be freely flowing, if that's any incentive."

Libby rolled her eyes. "I've sworn off. Trust me. But I'd love an invitation. Thank you."

"You've got it." He plucked a cell phone from his pocket and mere seconds later he was directing someone to put her on the guest list. "No, that's all right. Don't worry about the spelling right now. No address necessary," he said. "I'll deliver it personally."

For some odd reason his use of the word *personally* and the way he locked his gaze on her when he said it suddenly caused a tiny shower of sparks to cascade down Libby's spine. She took a quick gulp of coffee, hoping to extinguish them.

This guy was good, she thought. He was good not only with buildings, but with women, too. At least his technique seemed to be working fairly well with her at the moment. She swallowed the rest of the coffee.

She was so conscious of her sparkling, sizzling innards that she didn't even realize the painting contractor had walked up behind her until he cleared his throat rather loudly and said, "Here's your estimate, Ms. Jost. I guess you know it's a pretty big job, considering the age of the place and all. My numbers are there at the top,." He pointed with a paint-crusted fingernail. "You just give me a call whenever you decide."

"All right. Thank you so very much for coming. I'll definitely be in touch." She was thrilled—amazed actually—that he was willing to take on the work.

The man had turned and walked away as Libby

flipped a few pages to glance at the all important bottom line. Reading it, she could almost feel her eyes bulge out like a cartoon character's. She didn't know whether to scream or to faint dead away or to throw up—again—right there in the driveway. She might just do all three, she thought bleakly. This was terrible.

He wanted thirty-seven thousand dollars for all the painting and patching that needed to be done, which would leave her the not-quite-staggering sum of thirteen thousand dollars for additional, equally necessary repairs and renovations like plumbing fixtures, tile, carpeting, new beds and bedding and lighting, not to mention a bit of advertising and a new damn sign over the office door. She'd had no idea, none whatsoever, that her dreams were so damned expensive and so dreadfully, impossibly out of reach.

Libby was so stunned, so completely stupefied that she was only vaguely aware that David had taken the paper from her, and then the next thing she heard was a gruff and bear-like curse followed by the sound of tearing. Her painter's estimate, she observed, was now falling to the ground in little pieces, like an early, quite unexpected snow. It was a good thing she didn't want to hang on to it, she supposed.

"This is absolute bull," David said. "It's worse than highway robbery. I'm betting the guy doesn't even want the job, Libby, and that's why he jacked the price up so high. He probably just wanted to scare you off."

"Well, it sure worked," she said, trying to accompany her words with a little laugh. A very little laugh. "Gee, now I can hardly wait to see if the plumbing guy and the electrician try to scare me, too. I can imagine it already. It'll be just like Halloween here every day of the week. Trick or treat!" There was a small but distinct tremor in her voice that her sarcasm couldn't even begin to disguise. At the moment, quite frankly, Libby didn't care.

"Look," David said. "I can get my guys over here for two or three days or however long it takes. They can do the painting for you for a tenth of that amount. Even less than that, I'd be willing to bet."

"*Your* guys?" Libby's headache took the opportunity to make a curtain call just then. She closed her eyes a moment, hoping to banish the unwelcomed pain. "I don't understand this at all."

David was already opening his phone as he responded to her. "Painters. From the Marquis."

"But you're the architect." She blinked. "How can you…"

"Architect or not, I just happen to be the guy in charge over there right now," he said, sounding most definitely like a guy in charge.

"But…"

He snapped the phone closed and gave her a look that seemed to question not only her ability to make a decision, but her basic intelligence as well. "Look," he said. "It's really pretty simple. Do you want the painting job done, done well at a reasonable price, or not? Yes or no."

This was obviously a man who made lightning-quick decisions, Libby thought, while she tended to procrastinate and then a bit more just to be absolutely sure or, as in most cases, semi-sure. Procrastinating had its benefits, but maybe lightning quick was the right way to go at the moment.

"Yes," she said. "Yes, I do want the job done at a reasonable price. Actually, what I want is an utterly fantastic job at a bargain basement price."

"You'll have it," he said. He stabbed in a number, barked some commands that were punctuated here and there with curses, flipped his cell phone closed and then told her, "A crew will be here in twenty minutes. Write a list of everything you want them to do. And be specific."

Libby nodded. She could come up with a list for them in less than five seconds, she thought. Number One was *paint everything*. There was no Number Two.

While Libby worked on her list in the office, David walked around the shabby motel grounds once again, scowling, muttering under his breath, telling himself he must really be losing his grip. He'd just done one of the most stupid things in his life when he'd offered to help fix up the damnable place he had every intention of tearing down.

What was the old expression? Putting lipstick on a pig? He shook his head. There wasn't enough lipstick in the world for this dilapidated pigsty.

On the other hand, his crew of painters were on the clock anyway in case of last-minute problems before the Marquis' opening so this little detour across the highway wasn't going to cost him all that much. It wasn't about the money, though. It was more and more about the woman, the luscious little strawberry blond.

She'd already gotten under his skin just enough for him to fashion a lie about who he actually was. He'd introduced himself to her as the architect of the Marquis—an architect, for God's sake—a mere hired hand instead of the Big Deal Boss. That alone was enough to make him question his sanity.

He hadn't actually planned to do that or rehearsed any sort of deception, it had simply sprung forth somehow when she'd offered her soft, warm hand and then inquired, *And you are?* For a split second, while he held her hand in his, he hadn't been quite sure who he was, where he was or what he was doing.

He wasn't a liar, although he'd probably stretched or bent the truth a few times during business negotiations. But in his personal life, what little there was of it, particularly with women, he never lied and he never promised anything he didn't follow through with from the moment he said hello to a woman to the moment he said goodbye. And he'd said a lot of goodbyes in his time.

He'd spent year after year watching female faces and their accompanying body language abruptly change when they heard the name David Halstrom. It was like going from Zorba the Greek to Aristotle Onassis in the blink of an eye, again and again, year after year, woman after woman. Women looked at Zorba with curiosity and pleasure and genuine affection. They looked at Onassis as if they were seeing their own reflections in the window of a bank.

He was thirty-six-years-old now, and he'd been a millionaire since he was twenty-one and a gazillionaire for most of the last decade. But until he'd laid eyes on Libby Jost, with her strawberry-blond hair and her light blue eyes and the nearly perfect curves of her body, David hadn't realized just how much he'd truly yearned to be treated like a normal, everyday guy instead of a damn cash register.

So, what the hell. He'd be an architect for the next few weeks, and then he'd confess, and the fact that he had more money than God would go a long, long way in soothing Libby Jost's hurt feelings at his deception.

In the meantime, he decided he'd better be going before the painters arrived and greeted him by his actual name. He stopped by the shabby little office to tell Libby goodbye and to give her his private number just in case she needed him, and it was only then, when he actually said the words to her, that David realized just how much he wanted her to need him.

The painting crew turned out to be four young men in their twenties or early thirties, all of them in paint-splattered coveralls, and all of them with long hair tied back in ponytails and piercings in one place or another. They looked more like a rock band than a team of professional painters. She hoped David knew what he was doing as she gave them her list, walked them around the place, then waited for the bad news she had begun to expect.

"So," she asked when they'd completed their inspection of the place. "Can you do it? And for how much?"

She held her breath in anticipation of the bad news.

The tallest of the young men shrugged his shoulders and gave a little snort. "Well, it's a challenge, ma'am, no doubt about that. But, sure we can do it. Hell, yes. As for how much, as far as I know right now, you'll just have to pay for the paint. We're all on the clock over at the Marquis, so we get paid one way or another. Over here. Over there. It doesn't matter."

Libby was still holding her breath, waiting for the bottom line.

"I'm guessing seven hundred dollars ought to cover the supplies," he said. "Give or take a few bucks."

Then he pulled a fold-out palette of paint colors from his back pocket. "If you want to choose the main color and the trim right now, ma'am, we can pick it up and get started after lunch."

Libby was still a few beats behind him, still celebrating the seven hundred dollars, give or take, as if she'd just won the lottery. Things were suddenly, terrifically back on track, she thought, after this morning's horrible derailment.

"Ma'am?" He fanned open the color chart in front of her.

"Oh. Sorry." She looked at the chart. "Well, this won't be too hard. I've had these colors in my head for weeks. I want a rich, creamy ivory for the walls. This one. Right here." She pointed to a swatch. "And I want a deep, deep, wonderful green for the doors and the trim. There. That's it exactly. It's perfect."

"Cool," the painter said, then turned to his crew. "We're all set. Mount up, boys. Let's hit the road."

Libby hit the road, too, right after her ever reliable front-desk replacement, Douglas Porter, arrived.

She'd known him since she was two years old, and if her aunt Elizabeth was the mother figure in Libby's life, then Doug was most definitely her stand-in father after all these years. His nearly religious attendance at dozens of school plays and concerts and teacher's meetings, and his presence at every major event in her life more than qualified him for a special kind of parenthood. Plus, it was Doug who'd given her her very first camera on her tenth birthday, then spent hours showing her how to use it properly, not to mention forking over a small fortune for film, filters, lenses and often staggering developing costs.

But he wasn't really her uncle. He'd been the best man at Aunt Elizabeth and Uncle Joe's wedding and after Uncle Joe went missing in Korea over half a century ago, Doug simply stayed around. It was clear to anyone with eyes that he loved her aunt, and it never failed to sadden Libby that the two of them hadn't married.

"Elizabeth's pretty chipper today, Lib," he had announced when he entered the office. "You'll be glad to see that, I know. So what's going on around here? How many guests do we have?"

It had become a running joke between the two of them, about the guests, and she had offered the standard reply. "No more than you can handle, Doug."

She'd paused on her way out the door. "Oh, I'm expecting some painters this afternoon. They know their way around so you won't have to do anything."

"Painters?" His white eyebrows climbed practically up to his scalp. "Why on earth…?"

"No big deal," she said nonchalantly. "I'm just having them do a few touch-ups."

As she closed the office door she could hear him muttering something about throwing good money after bad, silk purses and sows' ears.

Libby was still smiling about that when she parked her car at the nursing home's rehab facility and walked down the long glossy hallway to her aunt's room. She knocked softly, then opened the door, happy to see that the crabby roommate wasn't there at the moment, but not so happy to see the sour expression on Aunt Elizabeth's face.

"Painters, Libby? You've hired painters? What on earth are you thinking, child?"

Libby sighed. "I guess Doug called." She should have figured on that, she thought, as she pulled a chair close to the bed. "I wish he hadn't done that. I wanted to surprise you, Aunt Elizabeth."

"I *am* surprised," she said, rearranging the sheet that covered her. "And not all that pleasantly, my girl. You shouldn't be throwing your money away…"

"Wait. Just wait a minute." Libby held up her hand like a traffic cop. Sometimes it was the only way to stop this woman from going on and on. "I got a very special deal on the labor, so the job really isn't costing much at all. Trust me."

Her aunt narrowed her eyes. "How much?"

"Seven, eight hundred tops."

"I don't believe you," she snapped.

"It's true, Aunt Elizabeth. Cross my heart. I'll even show you the canceled check when I get it."

The elderly woman clucked her tongue. "And I suppose it's already too late to stop this painting nonsense?"

"Yes," Libby said stubbornly.

Her aunt, equally stubborn, glared out the window for a moment before she snapped, "Well, then tell me what colors you picked out. You know very well that I don't like change, Libby, and when your Uncle Joe gets home he'll expect the place to look just as it did when he left for Korea."

After half a century he's not coming home, Libby wanted to scream at the top of her lungs, but she didn't. Aunt Elizabeth was an absolutely sane and reasonable woman, and likely a lot sharper than most folks her age, except for her complete and utter denial of her husband's death.

If you started to argue with her, if you tried to convince her the man was dead, she'd snap, "Well, then. Show me his death certificate." And of course there wasn't one since he'd gone missing in action, so her aunt always won the argument. And that was that.

When Libby was a little girl, she honestly believed her Uncle Joe would be coming home any day. She couldn't recall how old she was when Doug told her that the man had been missing in action since the 1950s. And he wasn't coming home. Ever. *Now, this is just between you and me, sweetie,* he had said.

Over the years, Aunt Elizabeth's friends and acquaintances tolerated this little lapse of sanity, this unreasonableness, or whatever it was. Doug, bless his heart, seemed to accept it completely. Libby did, too, she supposed, after all this time. When the subject arose, they'd all give her aunt the usual sympathetic nod or a brief *tsk-tsk* before quickly moving on to another topic of conversation.

Was she crazy? Perhaps. But the craziness was quite specific and limited to Uncle Joe and his imminent return. Aside from that particular bat in her belfry, Aunt Elizabeth was completely normal.

"Tell me the colors, Libby," her aunt demanded now.

"You're going to love them," she said. "I tried really hard to duplicate the original cream and green of the Haven View. I knew that's what you'd want."

"I must say that if I'd been in the mood to paint, honey, that's precisely what I would've chosen. And now I can't wait to come home and see it."

Libby nodded, feeling both deeply touched and hugely relieved in the same moment. At least her first surprise had ended well. Now there were approximately forty-nine thousand dollars worth of surprises still to come. Heaven help her.

Happily, there were no more surprises and no more ruffled feathers during the remainder of her visit. They had a good time together, and when Aunt Elizabeth's crabby roommate made her return appearance, Libby hugged and kissed her aunt goodbye and returned to her car. She was just fastening her seat belt when her cell phone rang.

David the Bear didn't waste much time, she thought. Hello was hardly out of her mouth when he asked, "Got any plans for this evening? What are you doing for dinner?"

"Hmm. Dinner." She tried with all her might to suppress a grin even though he obviously couldn't see it. And the answer she gave him wasn't all that far from the truth. "I was just now considering picking up a crisp domestic salad with a light Italian dressing and croutons, of course, while on my way home, then pairing it with delicately microwaved macaroni and cheese. Care to join me?"

"I've got a much better idea," he said.

Yes, he did indeed have a better idea, Libby thought when she finally closed her phone. Being chauffeured to a penthouse dinner at the magnificent Marquis most definitely trumped a take-out salad and lowly mac and cheese.

Three

The penthouse elevator door chimed as it swooshed open, and David, who'd been waiting in the marbled vestibule, turned to greet not the strawberry blonde he was expecting, but rather a luscious peach parfait. His heart shifted perceptibly in his chest and his entire body quickened at the sight of her. The woman looked utterly magnificent. If he'd felt merely smitten with Libby Jost before now, right this second he considered himself completely in lust.

She stepped forward into the vestibule, disclosing a delicate and adorable gold-sandaled foot along with a sleek and shapely length of calf. The pale peach fabric clung to her hips and her breasts, to her whole body like a second, shimmering skin. David swallowed hard. Just as he'd suspected, though, it didn't help all that much.

"Welcome to the Marquis," he said, striding forward and claiming her hand the way he wanted to claim every lovely inch of her from her tumbled hair to her golden toes. He couldn't help but think that her work put her on the wrong side of a camera.

"Thank you." She laughed then, a sound that was slightly husky and infinitely sexy. "I know I'm ridiculously overdressed," she said, "but I decided, since this will probably be my only visit here, at least to the penthouse, I might as well go all the way."

David clenched his teeth. He wasn't going to touch that remark with a ten-foot pole. Not even a twenty-foot one.

She blinked, and the color on her smooth cheeks deepened several shades, turning from delicate pink to a deep warm rose. "Fashion-wise, I mean."

Stupid, Libby chided herself. Even without the benefit of wine, she'd managed to put her foot in her mouth immediately upon her arrival. The man—quite gorgeous now and elegant in a black turtleneck and black pleated slacks—must think she's an absolute and unredeemable twit. She wrenched her gaze away from his face, let it stray around the suite and then immediately focused on the southern wall of floor-to-ceiling windows.

"What an incredible view," she exclaimed. "Oh, it's just amazing."

David reached for her hand. "Come have a closer look," he said, leading her into the suite, across a gorgeous oriental carpet that must've been the size of a football field and around burnished leather chairs and glass tables that gleamed richly in the ambient light. It was as if she'd landed smack in the middle of an issue of *Architectural Digest*.

As exquisite as the penthouse's décor was, the view from its enormous window was even better. Or so it seemed to Libby until her roving gaze practically skidded to a halt upon the scruffy landscape of the Haven View just across the highway. She'd never seen the place from so high, and it was not, she had to admit, a very pleasant sight. It was horrible, in fact. It was worse than horrible. The place was pure suburban blight.

The little guest cabins she'd been so thrilled about painting looked more like outhouses from this vantage point, and the glass globes of the lights along the driveway were so dusty and bug-splattered they barely seemed to shine at all. Squinting, she even decided that she could detect some rather significant damage to the shingles of a few cabin roofs, which was something she hadn't even thought to consider in her careful renovation budget.

It all struck her as utterly depressing, every feature, every shingle, every single square inch of the entire bedraggled place. Once again, she feared that her fifty thousand dollars wasn't nearly enough to bring the poor old motel up to speed. Not even a turtle's speed. She must've sighed just then or muttered something under her breath, because David, who was standing close behind her, touched her shoulder ever so gently and asked her what was wrong.

Everything, she thought, before she managed to put her game face back on as best she could, then turned to her host. "Well, the good news, I guess, is that the poor old Haven View will be hidden by leaves for eight or nine months every year from the guests of the Marquis. The bad news is worse than I imagined."

She waved a hand in front of her hoping to rid herself of these brand-new, unbidden feelings of despair. "I really don't even want to talk about it."

There was a small flicker of something close to sympathy or sadness in his expression for just an instant before he said, "Come on. Let's forget about the southern view for now." He clasped her hand in his once again. "Let me show you the really incredible views to the east and the west."

The east view was from a wide, slate-floored terrace with gorgeous wrought-iron furniture where Libby could easily imagine wearing an ivory satin robe with matching slippers while lingering over a late breakfast of croissants, sweet butter and strong Jamaican coffee. Right at that moment she could almost taste it.

"On a fine, clear day," he told her, "you can see the Arch." He pointed. "Right there. You'll have to come back sometime with your camera."

"I'd love to," she said. Oh, boy, would she love to. "I could get some really interesting shots."

A minute or so later, having gone from one gorgeous room to another even more gorgeous room, the promised view to the west was revealed when David pushed a button on a bedside console and a whole wall of drapery silently slithered back. Outside the exposed window, on the highway below, east-bound headlights shone like diamonds while west-bound taillights sparkled like a river of rubies, and she could actually see a bevy of stars twinkling in the dark sky above them all. It momentarily took her breath away.

Oh, how Libby wished she had her camera and a few specific lenses and filters just then to record it all. She wished she had a tripod in order to take a terrific time-lapse exposure of the traffic. Despite David's polite invitation a few minutes earlier, she doubted she'd ever be up here in the penthouse again.

"Does Mr. Halstrom have a place like this in all of his hotels?" she asked.

"More or less," he answered in a tone that struck her as rather brusque. "But when he's not in residence, his suites are all available to guests for the right price."

"Don't even tell me the price," Libby said. "I couldn't stand to hear it considering we try so hard to rent our dinky cabins for sixty-five dollars a day." Sadly, she thought, that economical price was probably far more than the accommodations were worth. Jeez. How long would it be before they might actually be forced to pay people to stay there, just for appearances sake?

"Maybe the new paint job will help," David offered, sounding vaguely unconvinced if not down-right disbelieving.

"Yeah. Maybe." She sighed. And maybe, she thought, maybe there were far more worthy recipients of her unexpected little fortune than the over-the-hill Haven View. Maybe she should reconsider the whole ridiculous endeavor. Like Scarlett O'Hara, she decided to think about that tomorrow.

Libby found herself forcing another smile then as she turned to her oh-so-handsome host. "Didn't you promise me a glass of red wine, David?"

The garnet-colored wine, French and positively ancient by her standards, was far and away the best that Libby had ever drunk. She sipped it cautiously, dreading a repeat performance of the night before, while David showed her the other rooms in this incredible place. The bathrooms alone were worth a hefty admission price.

Dinner arrived almost magically, wheeled into the suite on two shiny silver carts before being placed on the dining room table by two smartly outfitted waiters who gave the impression they were auditioning for a play, or perhaps a silent movie as neither one of them made so much as a sound above the clink of a water glass or the soft thud of a piece of heavy silver on the tabletop.

There were four different entrées to choose from, including a buttery salmon, a gorgeous filet mignon, lamb in an exotic mint sauce and roasted chicken with truffles that Libby ultimately couldn't resist. She was almost tempted to ask for a doggie bag in which to carry home the rejected dishes that the waiters promptly and silently wheeled away.

"Oh, what a terrible waste," she said with a sigh as she watched them turn a corner on their way to the elevator.

"Don't worry," David told her as he prepared to cut into his steak. "When that food gets back to the kitchen, it'll be devoured within a matter of seconds. The chef is working with a small staff prior to the opening while he refines the menu. I had him send up four choices because I didn't know what you might like. Feel perfectly free to be a critic. How's the chicken?"

"To die for," she said, reveling in her very first bite. "And the vegetables actually look edible which doesn't often happen where I come from."

She tried a petite, buttery carrot dusted with parsley and some other herb she couldn't identify, then rolled her eyes in delight. "Who knew a lowly carrot could taste so good? You know, David, your boss must weigh a ton if he eats like this every single day."

"Well, he works out a lot, I'm told," he said before taking another sip of wine and another bite of his filet. "I'd like to hear more about your photography, if you don't mind discussing it."

She didn't mind at all. It was probably her favorite subject and she was quite capable of going on endlessly about it, which she proceeded to do. But every time she politely—and curiously—attempted to change the subject and to inquire about him, David smoothly and affably turned the conversation back to cameras and lenses.

After dinner, they returned to the living room with its glorious window wall, where Libby avoided another painful glance at the shabby motel below. It was nearly midnight when she finally said, "I really should be getting back to Haven View. The man I left in charge, my uncle Doug, is almost eighty years old and really needs his rest."

David's left eyebrow quirked. "And you assume, I suppose, that your uncle has been overrun with demanding guests all the while you've been here?"

Libby had to hand it to him. The guy really did try to suppress his laughter even though he didn't quite succeed. She appreciated his sense of humor despite this particular, rather hurtful and annoying subject matter.

"You never know," she said with a little shrug of her shoulders before she stood up and extended her hand. "It was a truly lovely dinner, David. Thank you."

He stepped forward, smoothly brushing her hand aside as his arms reached out to encircle her. He gathered her close, kissed the top of her head, then her forehead, then the bridge of her nose. "I've wanted to do this all evening, Libby," he said, his breath warm and fragrant as expensive French wine on her face.

Libby felt like whimpering, *"What took you so long?"* But then David's mouth covered hers, and speech was suddenly and completely out of the question. She couldn't even think, but only inhale his wonderful scent and savor the rich remnants of wine on his lips. A tiny moan mounted in her throat, threatening to break loose and inform him just how much she craved his touch.

He leaned back slightly, used his thumb to angle her face up to meet his gaze. Those lovely hazel eyes of his had deepened to a dark and passionate green. "Stay here with me tonight. Don't go back to that dump."

Something clicked in her head, and Libby blinked

hard as her eyes began to focus again. She could feel her mouth flattening to a hard, thin line. Then she straightened up even as she took a step back, out of his arms.

"I don't want to be rude," she said, "especially after that divine dinner, and also because I truly like you, David. I like you enormously. But I won't have my aunt's lifetime endeavor trashed or made fun of. Not by you. Not by anyone." She paused a second, her eyes still locked on his. "I hope that's clear."

He nodded. "Got it," he said. He sounded absolutely sincere if not somewhat taken aback by her rather unexpected challenge. "I won't do it again."

"Good." Libby smiled. "I'm glad you understand." Then she lifted her chin and tapped a finger to her lips. "Now kiss me good-night again. Please."

Women rarely stood up to him, either professionally or privately. It was such a rarity, in fact, that David couldn't remember the last time it had happened. Hell, men rarely stood up to him these days. His little Libby was a tigress in peach silk. He smiled in the darkness at the memory of her fierce, flashing eyes, her stiffened spine and her delicate but formidable chin. More power to her, in fact. She'd had every right to put him in his place after he'd spoken disparagingly of her motel, wreck that it was.

He cursed himself now for deceiving this wonderful woman from the get-go. Had he ever had a more stupid, more self-defeating, almost suicidal idea? He was going to have to make it all right, but at the moment he didn't have a clue how to do it. All he knew was that he didn't want to lose her. Well, hell. He didn't even *have* her yet, but Lord how he wanted her.

He turned over in bed, pummeled the pillow once more with his fist, and eyed the bedside clock. It was two-fifteen. He'd be likely to wake her if he called her right now. With any luck, however, she'd be awake also, just across the highway, tossing and turning and thinking about him. Yeah. He should be so lucky.

Well, maybe he was. She answered her phone on the second ring.

David skipped the usual telephone introductions and niceties and immediately said, "Let's do something fun tomorrow."

A soft, sexy murmur came through the distance. "Like what?" she purred.

"I don't know. Let's just go somewhere, anywhere. We'll just hold hands and wander. We'll be kids on our very first date."

She laughed, and the sound was practically delicious. "I'll have you know," she said, "I sprained my ankle on my very first date."

"No problem. I'll carry you." David smiled in the darkness, imagining her in his arms. "Where should we go?" he asked her. "What about the zoo?"

"Been there."

"The art museum?"

She let out a long sigh. "Been there, too."

"How about the Arch?"

"Done that."

David, at a loss now, said, "Well, pick someplace. Anyplace. It doesn't have to be in St. Louis."

She was quiet a moment and then she said, "I know. Let's go to Hannibal."

"Hannibal?" David scratched his head. "You mean Hannibal, as in Tom Sawyer and Huck Finn?"

"Uh-huh. That's exactly what I mean. I haven't been there since I was a kid, and it's only an hour and a half or so away. I'll even drive if you'd like."

"Wait. I've got a better idea. Can you be ready to go by ten tomorrow morning?"

"Sure. I'm pretty sure I can get all my work out of the way by ten. Definitely by ten-thirty."

"Great. I'll send someone to pick you up then. Sleep well, darlin'. I'll see you at ten-thirty."

Then he closed his phone and, like a contented little boy who'd just had his warm milk and chocolate-chip cookies, David at long last drifted off to sleep.

On her side of the highway, Libby finally slept well, too.

Four

Early the next morning Libby taped a sign to the office door. Closed for renovations. She wasn't kidding herself that half a dozen or more cars would suddenly be turning into the motel's drive in search of accommodations, but the sign made her feel better anyway knowing her aunt Elizabeth would approve of properly informing the public. Libby was sure she could count on Doug to pass along the news when he visited her in the rehab facility.

The crew of young ponytailed painters from the Marquis had returned bright and early. Two of the cabins were already finished with their fresh coats of cream and deep green paint and they didn't look all that bad in Libby's admittedly biased opinion. After admiring them, she called a roofing company to arrange for an inspection of the damage she'd seen from the penthouse the night before. It wouldn't do any good to have brand-new décor, she figured, only to have it ruined by a leaky roof.

What else hadn't she considered? Libby wondered, when she'd budgeted her fifty-thousand-dollar gift? At the moment, she didn't even want to think about all the structural problems she might have breezily over-looked while concentrating on the place's worn and outdated décor. Strange and horrible visions of wood rot and mildew and termites began to tumble around in her brain, threatening yet another headache, some-thing she certainly didn't need this morning.

She looked at her watch and realized she had a little less than half an hour before she'd be swept off to the Marquis once again. Libby sighed, silently acknowledg-ing that her time would be better spent here, going over and adjusting renovation plans, than in Hannibal where she merely intended to have fun with a gorgeous guy.

It had been several years since she'd had the least bit of interest in a man, and now—faced with her fifty-thousand-dollar motel makeover challenge—along came David, who actually made her heart flutter while he gave her the impression that his own heart might be fluttering a little bit, too. How was that for terrible timing?

She showered, dressed and was ready to go without a moment to spare when the hotel's black limousine pulled into the drive. Jeff, the young man who had driven the limo the night before, opened the rear door for her. She thanked him, and then once he was settled up in front behind the wheel, she asked him, "How do you like working at the Marquis?"

"I love it," he said, his chin jutting over his shoulder in her direction. "It's a great place. Well, I guess you already know that."

"I do," Libby responded. "It's a beautiful building. Mr. Halstrom certainly hired the right architect."

"For sure. That Japanese team is tops."

Libby frowned. She had no idea that David was affiliated with an overseas company. He'd never mentioned it, and she had simply assumed he was a one-man operation, and a local one at that. It was probably a naive assumption in this day and age when everything and everyone seemed to operate on a global basis.

And then she wondered if David's permanent residence was in Japan, and, if so, just how soon he would be returning there. But then she decided she didn't want to know the answer to that particular question, at least not right now when she was looking so forward to their day in Hannibal, not to mention the night that might follow it.

Well, a girl could hope, couldn't she? She sank back into the luxurious leather upholstery. She didn't want to think about anything except the day ahead and the pleasure it might bring.

What she'd never anticipated, though, and never would have in a million years, was that David would have a helicopter on the roof of the Marquis, waiting to whisk them north along the Mississippi River.

"I've never been in a helicopter," she said more than a bit nervously as David boosted her inside it.

The rotors overhead were beginning to whirl and roar so he had to shout back. "Well, I've never been to Hannibal, Libby, so I guess that makes us even." He settled himself inside, then held her hand tightly as they lifted off into the bright blue sky. It wasn't much more than a minute or two before the big hotel appeared as just a shiny speck in the distance behind them.

The trip that would normally have taken them an hour and a half by car took them a mere thirty minutes in the air. The river town was busy, apparently preparing for a Huckleberry Finn festival, but since it was a weekday the tourists weren't exactly overrunning the place as they might have on a weekend. By a little past one o'clock, Libby and David had visited Mark Twain's boyhood home, ogled Tom Sawyer's white-washed fence and done a quick, fun trek through the museum, all the while holding hands like a couple of goofy kids. Like Tom and Becky, Libby thought.

For lunch they ordered hot dogs and fries from a street vendor, then carried their goodies down to the riverbank where they sat for an hour talking, watching as the Mighty Mississippi rolled by. As before, it was mostly Libby who talked up a storm while David listened and tended to deflect most of her questions back to her.

"Where were you born?" she asked him.

"Texas," he answered, raising his hand to dab a bit of mustard from a corner of her mouth. "What about you?"

"Here," she said. "Missouri." Then Libby spent a while talking about her parents' deaths, growing up at the Haven View and her aunt Elizabeth and Doug. As far as life stories went, hers wasn't very exotic. It wasn't even very interesting.

"Why did you want to be an architect?" she asked.

His answer was barely more than a shrug, followed by, "Why did you decide to be a photographer?"

Of course, having been asked about her favorite subject, she went into the whole story about her very first camera, her work at the St. Louis newspaper, and on and on.

She snapped pictures all the while—of the wharf, of the riverbank and the river—but hard as she tried, she wasn't able to capture David's face in a single frame. The man had an uncanny knack of turning, bending or lifting his hand at the exact moment she took the shot. She was almost beginning to believe he had some sort of camera phobia, and she so desperately wanted a picture of him, especially since he might be going to Japan at any time and she'd never see him again.

The mere thought of his leaving nearly made her queasy. She excused herself to return to Main Street for a bathroom visit. And then, smart little cookie that she was, she slipped a telephoto lens onto her camera while walking toward town, slowly turned and managed to get some really incredible shots of the man she'd left behind on the riverbank.

The gorgeous autumn day had turned cold late that afternoon, and by the time they climbed out of the helicopter on the roof of the Marquis, Libby was shivering.

"I know just how to warm you up," David said,

punching a number on his phone and telling whoever responded to have the hot tub in the penthouse ready in half an hour.

Then he led her to an elevator whose door swooshed open moments later just a few steps outside the cozy and dark little bar on the mezzanine.

"Two brandies, Tom. The good stuff," he said, holding up two fingers in the direction of the bartender who appeared to be presiding over an empty room.

"Right away, Mr...."

"Thanks," David said, cutting him off as he led Libby to a banquette in the corner where a candle glowed in the center of table.

She scooted into the lush leather seat. David slid in next to her and wrapped his arm around her shoulder. "You'll be warm in just one minute, darlin'. I promise."

She'd already warmed up considerably just from the heat of his body so close to hers. The subsequent brandy, in a huge crystal snifter, was hardly a match for her companion's warmth, she thought. And then Libby cautioned herself not to become too accustomed to the man or his warmth since it probably wouldn't be long before he was warming some other woman on the other side of the planet.

"I had more fun today than I've had in a long, long time," she said, lifting the brandy glass toward him. "Here's to my gracious and most gallant host."

The clink of the crystal when their glasses touched was a bit of music all on its own.

"Here's to Tom and Becky and Huck," he said. "And here's to you, Libby. I don't think I've ever had such a good time. Not even when I was a kid." He put the snifter down, and then his brow furrowed as he gathered in a long, deep breath.

It was one of those moments when a tiny little *uh-oh* sounded inside her head. Furrows and long, deep breaths were rarely, if ever, followed by good news. Furrows and long, deep breaths usually, almost always, meant trouble.

"Libby," he said softly, his eyes locking on to hers. "There's something that I…"

His cell phone let out a sharp little bleep just then. David cursed as he wrenched it from his pocket and very nearly broke it open in order to respond. "What?" he growled. After listening for a minute or so, he pressed a button to put the caller on hold. "I have to take this infernal call, Libby. I'm sorry, darlin'."

"Go ahead." Libby swirled the remaining brandy in her glass. The candlelight turned its color to a dark and lovely honey. "Take your time, David. I truly don't mind."

He kissed her forehead before he slid out of the booth, then walked—well, the man stalked, if truth be told—to the far end of the bar to continue the conversation. From her vantage point, and judging from his body language, it looked as if he were bestowing some very bad news on the person at the other end of the connection.

For the moment, Libby was just thankful it wasn't her.

David felt his mood darkening. Damn. He'd just had one of the best days of his entire life, but then business interrupted in the form of a threatened lawsuit by an irate guest in his London hotel, and his nervous Nellie of a British attorney felt obliged to alert him, personally, posthaste. David told the hysterical attorney if he ever called him again, he'd have him chained in the Tower of London, then drawn and quartered in front of Buckingham Palace with CNN given the exclusive rights to broadcast it live.

And now, to make matters worse, he'd be damned if he could locate something for Libby to wear in the hot tub. The little complimentary garments should have been stowed in a drawer in the penthouse spa, but it appeared as if someone—some soon-to-be former employee—had decided to stash hotel brochures, postcards and stationery there instead.

"It's all right, David," Libby said from her perch on the edge of the hot tub. "I can wear my bra and panties. It's not a problem. I've done it before."

The vision of her clad only in scanty silks, seethrough no doubt, beside some big gorilla in a hot tub didn't do a lot to lighten his current mood. He'd summon his assistant, Jeff, in a moment, no doubt ruining another of the man's dinners. But meanwhile he continued to search like a madman, cursing, slamming drawers and cabinet doors, and all the while berating himself for losing the opportunity to confess to Libby and tell her just who he really was. That, he well knew, was at the heart of his current furor.

Earlier, downstairs in the darkness of the bar, the words had been right there on his tongue, and he'd been ready to get down on his knees if he had to in order for her to forgive him. He wanted her that much. He was going to tell her now, even before their time in the hot tub. What sense was there in prolonging it? Hell. It wasn't as if he were going to confess to her that he was an axe murderer.

She would forgive him, wouldn't she? She had to, otherwise…

Just behind him then, Libby cleared her throat and uttered a whispery little *ta-da*.

He turned to see a vision of absolute delight, Libby clad only in feminine briefs and a snow-white lacey bra. Considering how great she looked when fully clothed, David couldn't even find words to describe her now. She grinned, and then pointed to the bubbling hot tub as she gave a pert little salute.

"Permission to come aboard, sir?"

David sighed inwardly. Whatever he'd intended to confess to her had suddenly flown right out of his head. And he had to admit that, even if he'd remembered, this was not the time to risk a confrontation. He might have been considered a liar under the circumstances, but he wasn't a downright fool.

"Permission granted," he said, quickly shrugging out of his own shirt and jeans, to join her in the warm caress of the water.

Settled chin deep in the wonderfully warm tub, feeling David's lean body right beside hers, Libby's eyes began to drift closed and she nearly fell asleep. How very strange, she thought, to feel so completely at ease with a man she'd only known for a mere two days. It wasn't like her to feel so relaxed with anyone, even after knowing them for months.

"I could stay right here for an entire week," she said, letting go of a soft and wistful sigh. "Maybe even a month."

He chuckled. "I don't know if I'd care to see you turn into a wrinkled, waterlogged prune, darlin'. I have to admit I like you just the way you are."

She turned her head toward him, gazing up at his face where the sexy smile lines had reappeared.

"Do you?"

Her voice was hardly more than a whisper, and even she could hear the longing in her tone. She couldn't help it. She adored this man, and she wanted him with every fiber of her being. If their coming together was fated to be only a brief affair before he went back to Japan, well, then, so be it. *Sayonara* to her dreams of the future. Libby decided to simply live in the present for now. Let the future take care of itself.

Perhaps it was the buoyancy of the water, but David drew her into his arms so effortlessly that Libby felt lighter than a feather. His lips were warm on hers, tender and wonderfully slow and sensuous. The touch of his tongue on hers was tender and exquisite. It seemed, just then, as if they had all the time in the world to explore and discover and make love to each other.

"You're perfect," he whispered. "But I already knew that from the first moment I saw you."

His hand moved to her breast, cupping it, a perfect fit for his smooth wet palm, a perfect distance to her nipple for his thumb to circle and explore. Libby gave a little shudder, and leaned her head back onto the rim of the tub as he covered her neck with languid kisses.

He murmured against her skin. "I've wanted this... I've wanted *you* from the moment I saw you clinging to that silly lamppost like a fallen angel."

"Emphasis on fallen," she said with a little sigh, then blew a puff of air upward to dislodge a damp stray curl from her forehead.

"No." His hand eased from her breast and then smoothed slowly, thrillingly down, over her hip to her inner thigh. "Emphasis on want. I want you, Libby. All of you. Now."

There was a great *whoosh* of water, and then she was high in his arms, clinging to his hard, wet neck as he carried her down a dimly lit hallway and into the bedroom where only the night before she'd watched the traffic flow like a river of jewels out the western window. He put her gently on the bed and left her for a brief moment to open a drawer, tear open a little square package, then returned to gather her into his arms.

"Tell me how to please you," he said, his fingertips drifting up and down her arm, setting off little shock waves of desire all over her. Then his hand strayed to her leg and the shock waves increased. "Anything you want. Anywhere."

Libby pressed closer to the hard length of his body, placing the palm of her hand to his cheek and tracing the now barely visible smile lines with her thumb. "Everything about you pleases me," she said. "I just want you. All of you."

They made slow, sensuous love while the diamond and ruby traffic lights flickered far below. In Libby's experience—which admittedly wasn't vast or all that recent—men tended to go for the gusto, returning to the lady's pleasure only after crossing the finish line alone. David, however, was in no rush at all. His every touch was leisurely, languid and absolutely divine. He seemed to have infinite pleasure in giving her pleasure.

Then it was Libby, when David at last entered her, who revved up the pace considerably, lifting her hips to meet each thrust of his, wanting almost desperately to capture all of him inside her and to keep him there forever. Their soft murmurs only moments earlier quickened to mutual groans of pleasure.

Everything in Libby's body curled tighter and tighter, wound up in itself, as she moved toward climax and then...

And then it felt as if her every cell suddenly let go in wave after wave of pleasure so intense she thought she might either laugh or cry or both. Within seconds, David followed her with a final powerful thrust, his whole hard body shuddering in his release.

They simply lay there then, locked in each other's arms, sated and waiting for their breathing to return to something that resembled normal, if indeed it ever would.

It was nearly nine-thirty before they could rouse themselves from the big bed on the west side of the penthouse. But when David heard a distinct and hungry rumbling coming from the direction of Libby's stomach, he reached for his phone and called downstairs. The chef, of course, had long ago retired from the kitchen, but an eager sous chef—now in line for a rather hefty raise, David decided—was more than happy to prepare his "special" omelette and a vegetable stir-fry.

When he turned to consult Libby on the meal, her eyes glittered like a wolf just spying a lamb.

"Send it up as quickly as you can," David told the sous chef.

They ate, quite ravenously, in bed. Libby wore a Marquis bathrobe, and with her tangled hair and her lips still flushed with his kisses, she reminded him of Venus, come to life right here in the Midwest.

"I should probably be getting back to the Haven View," she said after finishing one of the hotel's signature amaretto and chocolate-chip cookies.

David frowned. "I thought you said you put a sign on the door saying it's closed for the duration."

"I did, but…"

"Well?"

It seemed to dawn on her then that she had no other obligations, at least not at the motel, and there was no one to please for a change but herself. The notion apparently surprised her because she blinked and, for once, since the first time he'd met her, she appeared to be at a loss for words.

But David wasn't.

"Stay with me, Libby."

He brushed aside the silver trays, the empty dishes and the glassware, then drew her once more into his arms. "Stay."

And she did.

Five

When Libby got back to the Haven View at a little after nine the following morning, David's kisses continued to linger on her lips, on her throat, on... Well, everywhere. She felt such a warm and nearly tangible glow inside. It was like a fire that seemed to burn and caress at the same time.

By ten o'clock, however, the fire had fizzled out, most likely because of her tears. The roofing inspector had arrived, looked at all the cabin roofs and then handed her an estimate for forty thousand dollars plus tax.

"Keep in mind," he'd said while shaking his head, "that's just for the roofing, Miss Jost. It doesn't include the new gutters and downspouts this old place badly needs. Otherwise, you're going to see more damage in the future. You can count on it."

After he left, Libby walked inside the apartment behind the office and crumpled on the floor of the shower, letting the hot spray from above blend with her tears. It had been a long, long time since she'd wallowed in self-pity. The last, and probably the only other time she'd given herself permission to break apart, had been when she was ten years old and her cat, Joey, went missing. This morning she felt the way she had when she was ten, as if something so very close to her heart had just been run over or blown to smithereens.

She cried for a long, long time, until she had no more tears to shed, then she dried off, got dressed and went out to the main room of the office where she found Doug wearing his favorite and ancient St. Louis Cardinals sweatshirt while he flipped through a stack of mail. Funny, she thought. If her memory was correct, he'd been wearing a Cardinals T-shirt all those years ago when he'd consoled her about the loss of Joey.

"Morning, honey," he said cheerfully. "Did you have a good time in Hannibal?"

"I had a great time in Hannibal." Libby walked around to the other side of the desk, wrapped her arms around the elderly man's neck and planted a loud kiss on his balding head. "I love you so much, Doug," she said.

"Well, I love you, too, sweetheart." He chuckled. "But what'd I do to deserve such an enthusiastic greeting?"

She flopped onto the ratty floral couch across from the desk. "You were so sweet to me when my little Joey ran away."

Doug scratched his head with the sword-shaped

letter opener he'd been using. "Joey. Just a minute. Now let me think back. Was Joey the gerbil or the cat?"

Oh, jeez. She'd completely forgotten about George the gerbil who'd scampered beneath her bed one day, never to be seen again. Well, now she really was depressed.

"Joey was the cat," she said. "He was black with little white slippers on his feet."

"That's right." Doug's whole face seemed to sadden, every line and wrinkle turning downward. "I'm sorry about that, Lib. I remember. You were so unhappy, honey. I'm just glad I managed to soothe your heart a little bit."

Libby let out a long and weary sigh, thinking her heart could surely use a bit of soothing right now. When she was a little girl, she'd always gone to Doug for his comfort as well as his advice. He was patient and kind and incredibly smart. So why not seek his advice now, she wondered. She wasn't exactly doing a stellar job all on her own. She probably should have consulted him from the very beginning of this fifty-thousand dollar debacle.

"Doug…" she said, then hesitated. No, maybe it wasn't such a great idea. He'd tell Aunt Elizabeth every last detail and then all hell would break loose. Libby chewed on her bottom lip, still tender from last night's kisses.

"What, honey? What's bothering you?" Doug asked. "I know something is."

"Am I that transparent?" she asked.

"You are to me, kiddo. You always have been. Want to tell me what's up?"

Libby crossed her arms over her chest, feeling about

ten years old again and horribly vulnerable. "What's up, huh?" She forced a little half-embarrassed laugh. "Well, let's see. It's such a mess that I hardly know where to begin."

But somehow she began, first with the arrival of the mysterious check for the enormous sum.

Doug stopped her right there. "Wait. Hold it right there, Libby. You're telling me that somebody, some complete stranger, gave you fifty thousand bucks just because he liked your book about dying and dead motels? It was a wonderful book and all, but that's a hell of a lot of money just to say thanks for a good read."

"That's what I thought, too. I thought it was a joke at first. But the money's completely legitimate. The bank had no problem with it at all. There's fifty thousand dollars sitting in my checking account right now just waiting to be spent."

She followed that amazing bit of news by telling Doug of her hopes and dreams of using the money to revitalize the Haven View. She explained her carefully thought-out plans for both interior and exterior repairs, trying to be true to Aunt Elizabeth's original plans and color schemes.

When she got to the part about the painters, however, it was a bit tricky to maneuver around the facts because she wasn't really ready to disclose anything about David or her feelings for him. There was no sense complicating this with the mention of a lover who might not even be here in a week or two.

Finally, Libby concluded her tale with the staggering price of the roof repairs, and then lifted her hands helplessly and said, "I'm still not willing to give up this dream of mine, Doug, but I just don't know how to make fifty thousand dollars go the distance that's required. I just don't know if it's possible. I'd really, really welcome any ideas or suggestions, if you have them. But, please, please don't just tell me I'm crazy for wanting to do this."

Behind the desk, he closed his pale blue eyes a moment and pressed his lips together as if he didn't know what to say or didn't even want to respond at all, which Libby could easily understand. It was her money, after all, and therefore her problem. And she'd certainly made a mess of it so far.

Then Doug cursed gruffly, something he rarely did, before he curled one hand into a fist and pounded the desktop with it.

"Dammit, Libby. I wish you'd come to me, to both of us right off the bat. I know you meant well making it a surprise, but your aunt Elizabeth and I are way too old for surprises, honey. We like to know what's what. We *need* to know. It's pretty important at our age," he muttered. "We really need to be kept inside the loop instead of outside in the dark."

Libby sighed. Doug was absolutely right. She should have informed them. She wished that she had.

"Well, now you know. *What's what* is fifty thousand dollars is burning a big hole in my pocket. And now that you know about it, you can help me do this right, Doug, if it's at all possible." She narrowed her gaze on his face. "Is it possible? Or is it just a silly and impossible dream? Tell me the truth."

He leaned back in his chair, then rubbed his hand slowly across his white-whiskered chin before he spoke. "That's a generous thing you want to do for her, Libby. I think your aunt Elizabeth will be thrilled as all to get-out to see this old dump looking the way it did in the old days. It's been hard on her, watching the place go to seed the way it has over the years."

"Oh, I know," Libby said. "And I so desperately want to change all that. I want to make her really happy."

"I know you do, sweetie." Doug sighed. "But fifty thousand dollars, as grand a sum as it is, just isn't going to cut it. Not with prices like they are today, and not with all the repairs we're in need of around here. Your fifty thousand dollars, honey, is hardly a drop in the bucket." He shook his head so very sadly. "I'm afraid it can't be done, Libby. Not unless you're a magician or that secret admirer of yours plans to add a million or two to his original gift."

Libby dragged in her lower lip and bit down on it, trying with all her might not to give way to another flood of tears. What good would they do?

"Unless…" Doug leaned forward in his chair.

"What? Unless what?"

"Ever heard that old expression, Libby, about there being more than one way to skin a cat?"

She nodded, wondering what in the world he was getting at and why he was smiling all of a sudden when everything seemed so horribly, bitterly bleak. He looked like a damned Cheshire cat, and she wanted to skin *him* at the moment. "What?" she pressed. "What are you thinking?"

"Do you remember the work I did a while back for Father James O'Fallon when he was organizing his halfway house and homeless shelter?"

Again, Libby nodded. She remembered it well. Doug had volunteered his time as an accountant to help the energetic young priest acquire an affordable facility and to properly set up his charitable organization. That had been years ago, but the place—Heaven's Gate—was still doing wonderful work by providing food and shelter and hope to those who lacked all three.

"Just what are you getting at, Doug?"

"I drive into the city to visit that place pretty often, you know. Mostly just to chew the fat with Father James. He's a bigger Cardinals' fan than I am, and that's saying something."

"But what does that have to do with Haven View?" she asked. She had absolutely no idea where he was going with this.

"There's a new program at Heaven's Gate," he said. "It just started a couple months ago. They're training some of their people to work in the trades. Painting, carpentry, plumbing, things like that."

Now a little bulb started to glow above Libby's head as she suddenly saw just where he was going. "All the things we need done here," she said.

Doug nodded. "Yep. We need the work done and I can promise you that Father James needs fifty thousand dollars. What do you think, honey?"

Libby stood up so fast she nearly fell over. "My God! I think you're a genius, Doug. That is just inspired. Can we drive downtown right now and talk to him?"

The elderly man laughed. "I guess with that Closed sign on the door we can leave any time we want, Libby. Let me just give the good father a call."

Across the highway, high above it in the penthouse, David was just getting out of bed at eleven-fifteen. He'd gotten up a few hours earlier to see Libby safely off with Jeff, his reliable chauffeur and assistant and then Jeff had immediately returned to see what else the boss needed done.

"I haven't had time to go through all the Haven View documents yet," David told him while trying to stifle a yawn. "Anything I should know about the situation right now? Anything about it that can't wait a couple of hours?"

Jeff shook his head. "I think it'll keep. I probably shouldn't say this, Mr. Halstrom, but you look like you could use a few more hours of sleep."

He usually maintained a fairly stern demeanor with his employees, but David couldn't help but laugh at the remark. "I'm getting too old for this," he said.

"Well, perhaps it's time to settle down, boss. Or at least to think about it."

The kid rarely, if ever, made personal observations or remarks. A few days ago such comments might've earned him a dark, scathing look and a swift verbal reprimand. Today, however, David felt much too mellow and too downright happy to do anything but say, "Maybe you're right, kid. Maybe you're right."

Now, after a few hours of sleep, he felt somewhat restored, but that little thread of giddiness and gladness was still there inside him. Instead of his habitual Grinch demeanor, he felt almost like a little boy on Christmas morning, and that was some kind of first, he decided, because even when he was a little boy, there wasn't much giddiness or gladness in him. None, if truth be told.

"Libby, Libby," he muttered into the mirror while he shaved. "What the hell are you doing to me?"

After he showered and dressed, he punched her number into his cell phone. She'd written it down for him before leaving, but now he couldn't remember if it was her cell or the front desk at the crummy motel. Either way, there was no answer, which made him feel a little sad and lost for a moment, until feeling sad and lost made him feel like a real jerk.

So, he proceeded to call the Halstrom home office in Corpus Christi. Surely there would be somebody there he could yell at in order to drive this sappiness out of his system.

Once Libby and Doug were downtown, she asked him if he'd mind if they stopped at the newspaper's office for a minute so she could drop off some film for developing. Leave of absence or not, she'd become incredibly spoiled by the paper's freebies. Most newspapers had gone completely digital these days, but the St. Louis paper, out of nostalgia perhaps or pure laziness, still maintained a small, cramped and cobwebby darkroom.

Inside the building, she didn't want to waste time so she tried hard to avoid people she knew—and there were so many of them—as she made her way to the northwest corner of the third floor where her good pal, Hannah Corson, was on duty, looking harried and hassled as always. Libby plucked several film cans from her handbag.

"Can you run these for me, Hannah? No rush, but it'd be wonderful to have the prints in two or three days."

"Sure. No problem." Hannah took the film cans and promptly stashed them on a shelf in a little metal box labeled "To Do." "So, it's good to see you, Libby. How's everything going out at the Weary Traveler?"

Libby couldn't help but laugh. Her coworkers must've come up with a few hundred alternate names for the Haven View in the past decade, most of them rather risqué if not downright X-rated. A few brave souls had even come out to spend the night in one of the little cabins, and although they all claimed to have enjoyed the experience, she noticed nobody ever made a return engagement.

"Everything's going great," she said, surprised that she actually meant it.

"How 'bout hanging around and having lunch with me?"

"Thanks, Hannah, but Doug's waiting for me downstairs."

"Okay. Well, I'll give you a call when your prints are ready. Probably day after tomorrow. I'm backed up here for the Sunday edition. You know how it is. I miss your nice, crisp black-and-white shots, Libby."

Already at the door on her way out, Libby blew her a kiss. "Thanks, Hannah. I owe you. Again."

"Yeah, yeah, yeah. Everybody owes me," the woman grumbled. "I really should change my name to Hannah Kodak, I guess."

When she got back to the street, Doug had moved to the driver's seat of her ancient minivan. "Hop in, Libby," he said, starting the engine. "Come on. Shake a leg. We're already ten minutes late."

She hopped in, and immediately reached for the seat belt to yank it across herself and fasten it tight. Doug had always been a very creative driver, and now that he was in his late seventies, he didn't seem to feel the rules of the road applied to him personally. She held her breath as they whizzed three blocks north and then two blocks west to the Heaven's Gate facility.

For all the time Libby had spent at the newspaper's office these past years, she rarely visited the adjacent area to the north. Little wonder, because there wasn't much there except crumbling, boarded-up buildings and vacant lots filled with weeds and every kind of trash imaginable. Ever since finishing her book about down-and-out motels, she'd been hoping to be struck by an idea for another book.

It occurred to her now that there was a strange, haunting, even terrible beauty in all this urban decay. There was a burned-out church on a corner that almost seemed to be begging her for a series of photographs. Libby filed the notion in the back of her brain, hoping that once the repairs were accomplished at the motor court, she'd have time to pursue the concept.

Doug whipped the minivan into a small gravel parking lot, hit the brakes and skidded to a stop, then turned off the engine. "Here we are, Libby, my girl. Let's go. We don't want to keep Father James waiting all afternoon. He's a very busy guy."

As she climbed out of the vehicle, she remembered to check her cell phone for messages. Good grief. There were a half-dozen calls, all of them from David. She didn't know whether to feel flattered or alarmed. Well, emergency or not, he'd simply have to wait until she met with Father James. The fate of the Haven View seemed to be hanging in the balance of this quickly arranged meeting. She couldn't allow anything to distract her.

Not even David.

Six

After their meeting and a brief tour of Heaven's Gate, Father James walked Libby and Doug out to the parking lot. The priest had listened intently to their proposal and seemed to be fascinated by it even though the fine points hadn't been worked out yet. In all honesty, the plan was barely past the light bulb over the head stage, but Libby and Doug had been eager and enthusiastic in their presentation, if not burdened by the details. Obviously the fifty thousand dollars provided Father James with more than a little incentive to take it under consideration.

"I'll present it to my board of directors when we meet early next week," he told them. "And I expect they'll be equally intrigued and enthusiastic."

Libby tried hard to hide her disappointment at the delay. "I don't suppose you could do it any sooner."

He gave her a patient, practically angelic smile, one he must've used a hundred or more times a day in this facility, and then he shook his head. "I'm afraid not."

"That's plenty soon," Doug said. "And remember, both of you, we still have to present this plan to Elizabeth, and Lord only knows—pardon me, Father—how she'll respond. She can be downright cranky and stubborn as all get-out sometimes."

Libby rolled her eyes.

Father James gazed heavenward a moment, then said, "Well, I've been known to get cranky and stubborn myself. If this is meant to be, my friends, it will happen. Perhaps we should simply leave it at that for the time being."

Easier said than done, Libby thought on the drive home. It wasn't going to be so easy for her to put the brakes on her big plan, even if only until next week. Now which one of them was going to make a heartfelt presentation to Aunt Elizabeth, she wondered.

Afternoon westbound traffic was fairly light, so she used her right hand to flip open her cell phone which now registered two additional calls, both of them from David. Libby couldn't help but smile. Persistent fellow, her handsome architect, wasn't he? And, oh my, she thought, how she adored it.

Doug pointed to her phone. "That wouldn't be your new suitor, would it, Libby?"

She nodded.

"I'm looking forward to meeting him."

Libby laughed. "Well, as Father James would say, *All in good time, my dear Doug. All in good time.*"

* * *

As it turned out, Libby didn't have to return David's calls. He was waiting at the Haven View—arms crossed and one hip lodged against his Jag—when she and Doug got back.

Libby's heartbeat immediately picked up speed. How was it possible, she wondered, that this man looked better, more handsome and even more desirable every time she laid eyes on him? At this rate, she would surely go into cardiac arrest at the mere sight of him in a week or so. She could only hope that she caused a similar, significant drumbeat inside his hard-carved chest.

By the time she'd parked the minivan in back of the office, he was standing next to the driver's side door, reaching out to open it.

"Hey," she said, sliding from behind the wheel and practically into his arms. "I was just going to call you."

"So you got my calls?"

She laughed. "I got them all. Yes. They very nearly melted my cell phone."

"I missed you."

Well, jeez, now, in addition to her phone, he was melting her heart. "I'm glad," she said softly. "I missed you, too. Hey, I want you to meet somebody very special to me."

By now, Doug had climbed out of the passenger side of the van and was walking toward them, looking once again like a grinning Cheshire cat.

"Doug, I'd like you to meet David," she said. "David, this is Doug, the very best father in the world."

They shook hands, and Doug immediately said, "I've heard a lot about you, young man. Libby tells me you designed that gorgeous building across the street."

David lowered his head and consulted the pebbles beneath his feet for a moment before he said, "Yes, sir."

"Well, let me congratulate you." Doug angled his head northward. "She's a real beauty."

"Thank you, sir."

"I'll leave you two alone. I never did finish up today's mail in the office so I guess I better get to it." Doug kissed Libby's forehead, then turned to walk away.

"Nice guy," David said softly.

Libby nodded. "Yes, he is."

"I really did miss you today." He reached out to touch the back of his fingertips to her cheek.

There was a slightly yearning quality to his voice that Libby had never heard before, and judging from the expression on his face, he really had missed her.

"Good," she said. "I'm glad you did."

"Come back to the hotel with me," he said, pulling her into his arms and burying his face in her neck. "We can play in the hot tub again, and then see what else the kitchen can come up with for our dinner."

Libby made a little humming sound deep in her throat. "That sounds divine, but..."

He lifted his head. "But what?"

"I just hate to leave Doug alone this evening."

"Is he ill?"

"Oh, no. Nothing like that. The man's healthy as a horse. It's just that we're working on this wonderful idea, and there's so much to discuss."

"What sort of idea?" he asked.

"Well…"

Just then Doug walked around the rear corner of the office, jingling a set of car keys in his hand. "I'm off to see Elizabeth now, Libby. I'll probably stay there and have supper with her while I tell her about today. If you don't need me back here, I'll just go on home afterward, honey."

"Give her my love," Libby said. "And let me know what she says, Doug, will you? As soon as you can."

"Will do." He appeared only a bit stiff and awkward as he angled into the driver's seat of his old Pontiac. "Nice meeting you, David," he said just before turning the key in the ignition.

"Hope to see you again, sir," David responded before he smiled down at Libby. "Looks to me like somebody's a free woman this evening."

The free woman laughed, a luscious sound if ever David had heard one, then took his hand to lead him around the office and into the center of the pebbled drive. The place was deserted. As it should have been, David thought.

Libby made a broad and sweeping gesture with her arm.

"Pick a cabin, my dear. Any cabin," she said. "Or choose a number between one and six."

"What?"

"Choose a cabin, David. We've got the whole place to ourselves." She grinned up at him. "My personal choice would be Three, since it's my lucky number, not to mention the fact that the shower in there still works pretty well."

David decided that his brain was probably operating inefficiently because his bloodstream was shunting its contents below his waist at the moment. She wanted to make love here, in this squalor, rather than in the silk sheets and wall-to-wall splendor of the Marquis across the street? Make love *here?* Was she nuts?

Maybe the better question from David's point of view was could he even perform here under the circumstances, knowing he was making a concerted effort to acquire the crummy Haven View in order to tear it down.

Early this afternoon, after going through the paperwork, he'd sent Jeff, in the guise of a real-estate investor, to pay a visit to Libby's aunt Elizabeth in the rehab facility, where he had offered the woman whatever price she wanted for the place. "Name your price," Jeff had told her mere seconds before the old lady called the front desk to have this shady weasel escorted from her room.

Having struck out with Aunt Elizabeth, David then opted for plan B, and had directed Jeff to prepare a statement for the municipal council, requesting this acreage to be officially designated as blighted, and thus eligible for condemnation and immediate demolition.

The proposal to the municipal council also included the Halstrom's promise to develop the condemned property, its subsequent usage to be determined at a later date. Jeff was probably working on the document right this minute, dotting *i*'s and crossing *t*'s.

David let go of a long sigh. It wasn't that he didn't know he was working at cross purposes with Libby, but suddenly his deception hit him quite physically. He could feel his erection withering at the mere thought of Libby's reaction to this news. She'd hate him for it. And the sad fact was that she'd have every right to hate him.

"I need to make a quick call," he said, reaching for his phone, then flicking it open and hitting Jeff's number. "This will only take me a minute."

She was still smiling when she said, "Well, you better make it fast, mister, or else I reserve the right to choose the cabin."

He tried to smile back, but his face felt nearly frozen. When Jeff picked up the call on the third ring, David said simply, "Stop working on the current project. I'll get back to you about it later. Understand?"

Jeff uttered a surprised, almost strangled yes, then David snapped the phone closed and dropped it back into his pocket.

"Project?" Libby's lovely face was turned up to his, curiosity sparkling in her blue eyes. "Are you working on another hotel, David?"

"Something like that," he said, finally managing to smile. "But at the moment, my love, I'm working on something much more important."

"What?" she asked.

"This."

He gathered her up, held her closely against his chest, and said, "Show me the way to lucky Number Three."

* * *

Libby lingered in the shower, almost too embarrassed to leave the bathroom and face David. Had she ever had a worse idea in her entire life? Why would anyone ask the man responsible for the mirrored and glorious piece of architecture across the highway, the man who'd wined and dined her in its glorious penthouse, to even set foot in this chamber of horrors? What had she been thinking?

The door had opened with a long, drawn-out squeak comparable to a Boris Karloff movie, and then, as they stepped inside, the powerful odor of pine and Lysol had smacked both of them in the face. David, bless his heart, had tried not to cough, but it wasn't possible. Libby herself had had an immediate sneezing fit before running into the bathroom and locking the door.

Now, the fluorescent light over the sink was making an odd, erratic buzzing sound and the toilet, just to the right of the tub, gurgled every once in a while even though she hadn't used it. The plastic shower curtain, with its sand dollars and starfish and various ocean flora, looked so pitiful hanging there that Libby had to keep her eyes closed most of the time she was in the shower.

For one grim and painful moment, she decided that tearing this whole wretched place down was the obvious and only solution. Surely she could make her aunt Elizabeth see that.

But then she knew it was impossible. Aunt Elizabeth, as always, would stand her ground—this ground—her precious turf—the same way she always did when she insisted that Uncle Joe would soon be coming home. Libby couldn't make her change. Lord knew Doug hadn't been able to change her in all their decades together.

When all was said and done, there really wasn't much Libby could do other than go with the flow. And the flow right now, coming down from the shower head, seemed to be welling up in the tub because of a drain that wasn't working properly. She swore under her breath, then yanked the faucets off, hardly caring at the moment if she broke them or not.

She grabbed a towel—thin from years of wear and washing—and did her best to dry off. After raking her fingers through her damp hair, she wrapped the ratty towel around herself and opened the door.

David was sitting on the edge of a twin bed, leaning forward to change channels on the small television, something he probably hadn't done in years.

"Welcome to 1970," Libby said only half in jest. "Do you feel like you're in a time warp? Like you've been transported back several decades?"

"Nope," he answered as he punched off the television, then reached out his arms toward her. "I feel like Prince Charming waiting for his Cinderella."

"David," Libby said softly, hugging her towel tightly around herself. "I'm truly sorry that I insisted on this. I have no idea why it seemed so important to me, but I'm ready to leave, this very minute, if that's what you'd prefer."

He stood, and then took several strides across the gold shag carpet, closing the distance between them. "Actually, I'd prefer to make love to you, Libby darlin'. Here. Now."

She tilted her head up, passed the tip of her tongue across her lips, inviting his kiss. Craving his kiss. "Yes," she said. "Here. And right now."

What did it matter *where* she was, she thought, when David's kisses made her forget *who* she was. She released her grip on the damp towel and let it drop to the floor.

David stepped back. Without even touching her, he ravished her with just his eyes, whose color had deepened to a dark forest green. And his gaze alone caused Libby's stomach to clench with a ravenous hunger, as if she hadn't eaten for weeks. She'd never wanted a man the way she wanted this one. She never even knew, in all her thirty years, that such all-consuming desire was possible.

As he had before, David loved her slowly, exploring every part of her body as if she were the first woman he'd ever encountered, while leading her to discover sensations she'd never felt before.

And as before, it was Libby who, when pushed to the edge by his slow hands, by his warm tongue, by the feel of him so hard and deep inside of her, pulled David with her for the long tumble through magnificent fireworks and bright shooting stars.

Libby let herself drift into sleep, thinking she never wanted this man to leave her. If he did, she just might have to follow him if it meant going to the ends of the earth.

Seven

When Libby offered to fix dinner for him—which translated to popping two cartons of frozen macaroni and cheese into the microwave and seeing what she could come up with for a salad from the contents of the fridge—David politely declined, then offered a far better solution to the problem of dinner.

"Let's go across the street."

Libby laughed. "I thought you'd never ask."

He didn't take her up to the penthouse this time, but rather directly into the Marquis' shining new, state-of-the-art kitchen, where the sous chef who'd fed them so well the previous evening was still on duty.

The young man snapped to his feet the moment they walked in.

"How're y'all?" he said, revealing a wide smile along with a southern accent.

"We're fine," David answered, "and we're famished. Mind if we look around?"

"It's your kitchen. Whatever you find, sir, I'll be more than happy to prepare. Kitchen's are way better for cooking in than for sitting around in."

David took Libby's hand and led her deep into the inner workings of the facility. She'd never been in a restaurant kitchen before, and it was a whole new world for her.

"I'm not a very good cook," she confessed while gazing into a huge stainless-steel refrigerator that was crammed with things she couldn't even identify.

David, close beside her, chuckled. "So I gathered."

"My aunt Elizabeth isn't either." She sighed.

"Maybe it's genetic," David said, his lips sliding into a grin and his eyes nearly twinkling. "What looks good to you? Anything strike your fancy?"

Actually nothing looked good because it wasn't cooked, and there were no pictures to consult for the final product. "You choose for us, David," she said. "As an old mac and cheese girl, I'm more than willing to defer to your expertise."

He called out to the sous chef, naming ingredients and spices and sauces that might have been Martian as far as Libby knew. Then he told him, "We'll be in the bar. You can serve us in there."

As they left the kitchen, Libby saw David slip a bill from his pocket, fold it discretely, then place it on the table in front of the young cook.

"That's really not necessary, Mr...."

David cut him off. "Take it. It's my pleasure."

"Thank you, sir."

She glimpsed a corner of the bill in passing—a whopping hundred dollars—then tried to recall the biggest tip she'd ever bestowed on someone. Last year, she thought, two days before Christmas she'd ordered a pizza and the delivery guy had nearly fainted when she'd given him an extra twenty. She wondered now if he might actually have passed out if she'd given him a hundred.

David's hand was warm on her back as they entered the dimly lit bar. He lifted his other hand to signal the bartender.

"Two Merlots," he said. "The 2004s."

"Yessir."

Libby slid into the same soft leather booth where they'd sat before. It was beginning to feel comfortable. Probably too comfortable, she thought. With any other man she would have been content to enjoy the here and now, never giving a thought to tomorrow or next week, and certainly not worrying about the next year. Her intense feelings for David, however, were making her contemplate the future and that made her feel horribly vulnerable.

He settled beside her, draping his arm around her shoulders, his thigh wedged against hers. "It won't be this quiet here in a little less than two weeks. In fact, it'll be hard to find even a single seat in here."

"Well, that's good, isn't it?"

"Good for the hotel," he said. "But it sure puts a

cramp in our style, Libby. I'm enjoying having the place all to ourselves. What about you?"

"I am, too," she said. "Of course, there's always Cabin Three."

"Not if I can help it," David said, one eyebrow arching just as the bartender approached with a bottle of wine and two glasses.

He aimed the dark bottle perfectly toward David, allowing him to see the label and give a nod of consent before he proceeded to open it, almost magically with a corkscrew and to pour a bit into a glass. David tasted it, then nodded, after which the bartender filled both their glasses.

They'd barely taken their first sip of the rich red wine before the sous chef was sliding a gorgeous salad, edged with fat purple grapes and orange slices, in front of them. He added two salad forks, two stiff linen napkins and a small basket of peppered croutons before he disappeared back into his kitchen.

Libby took another swallow of wine, then set her glass down and said, "Do you know what impresses me the most about this hotel?"

"No," he said. "Tell me."

"The fact that everyone who works here, at least everyone I've seen so far, appears to be ridiculously happy. That's just not normal, David. In my experience, most of the people who work in hotels are crabby if not downright glum."

"Well, I suspect it's because the place hasn't opened yet, and the work schedule is still relatively light. But the Halstrom hotels haven't had many complaints about their staff. They're paid well above the normal scale for hotel workers."

"I wish I could say the same for the Haven View where we all work for free."

Libby picked up her fork to try the salad just as two women appeared in the entrance of the bar. Both of them were absolutely stunning, as if they'd just stepped out from a page of a fashion magazine. The statuesque blonde wore gold bracelets up to her elbows and pencil-thin jeans with leather boots that went all the way to her knees. The brunette beside her sported a long suede skirt, a to-die-for fur jacket and a pair of open-toed pumps with what seemed like six-inch heels.

Libby could hardly take her eyes off of them, but she managed to just in time to see the bartender flick his hand in their direction as if to signal them to leave. At nearly the same moment David began to punch numbers into his cell phone while swearing under his breath.

"Get down here. The bar. Now," he said before snapping the phone closed and breathing one more curse.

"What in the world is going on?" she asked.

He glared at the brass and glass door of the bar as if he were trying to melt it. "Hookers," he said.

"Oh."

She looked again at the two incredibly beautiful women poised in the doorway, then back at David.

"How can you tell?" she asked, her voice barely more than a whisper, as if she wouldn't want the two women to overhear. As far as Libby knew, the only "working girls" she'd ever seen were on television and in the movies.

Before David could answer her question, the sous chef reappeared, balancing a large round tray shoulder high. At the sight of the beauties in the doorway, it was all he could do to keep hold of the tray while still maintaining his own precarious balance. China and silverware clattered madly as he maneuvered the tray to an adjacent table just in the nick of time.

"Looks like the Marquis is officially on the map, sir," he muttered as he set the plates in front of Libby and David. "What can you do, eh? It was just a matter of time."

David's only response was another guttural curse.

"Enjoy your meal," the chef said, taking one last, lingering look at the visitors before disappearing back into his kitchen.

Gazing down at her dinner, Libby didn't have the vaguest idea what it was although it truly did look like a work of art. She was about to ask David what he'd ordered for them when the elevator door chimed and opened, revealing Jeff, her limousine driver, who stomped out to confront the two women.

What he did, actually, was smile broadly as he looped an arm around each of their shoulders, somehow effortlessly turning them away from the bar and toward the main hotel entrance. Only seconds later he and the women were out of sight.

"That was my driver," Libby said, somewhat astonished. "That was Jeff."

"He obviously moonlights as a bouncer, and a damn

good one, too," David responded, sounding at least fifty degrees cooler than he had a few moments ago. "Try your sea bass. It's delicious."

So that's what was on her plate, Libby thought. She picked up her fork and tried a tiny bite, only to discover that it was indeed delicious. Still, she could have done without the brussels sprouts, even though they did look beautiful.

It was over a brandy after dinner that Libby told him about her *absolutely amazing* plan for the motel. All the while David listened, he hoped his face wasn't betraying his feelings, which at that particular moment were bordering on panic and possible murder.

Now— Now—! she wanted to bus in a small army of convicted felons to work across from the Marquis every day. She might as well have said she'd arranged for a chain gang dressed in black and white stripes to pick up trash in front of his hotel. If he hadn't known better, he would've thought she was deliberately trying to drive the Halstrom Corporation out of business, at least here in St. Louis.

"It's a terrific idea, isn't it?" Her face was glowing, only partly from the brandy. "The motel gets a total makeover and Father James's clients get the experience they need. Everybody wins."

Except me, David thought. And he stood to lose millions upon millions, not to mention the deleterious effect on his company's reputation.

"Have you run this past anybody yet?" he asked her. "An attorney? Or someone on the town council?"

She shook her head. "It's still a bit early. Father James's board of directors doesn't meet until next week."

"In my experience," he said, "boards are more than willing to argue a single decision for several meetings, even the insignificant ones."

Libby took another sip of her brandy, then sighed. "And then, of course, there's Aunt Elizabeth who could kill the whole deal with a single 'no.' Doug was supposedly talking to her about it this afternoon, but since I haven't heard from him, I suspect he chickened out."

"Smart guy," David said. "You'll need to increase your insurance coverage to the max, you know, considering who'll be on the motel property. You'll need at least several million in liability coverage, just for openers."

"I hadn't even thought about that."

And that's what David was counting on. The sooner he could toss a monkey wrench into this latest plan of hers, the happier he was going to be.

"Well," he said, "no sense even thinking about any of the details until all your ducks are in a row."

Dead ducks, he dearly hoped.

In the lobby outside the bar David wrapped his arms around her, nuzzled his face into her neck, and then whispered, "So, my place or yours?"

Libby sighed. It had been such a long day, and as much as David was moving into her heart, he was also an incredible distraction at the moment from the things she needed to do as far as the Haven View was concerned. She tilted her head back, and it pained her to see that his smile had already been extinguished in anticipation of her response.

"Come home with me," she said softly. "I'm not guaranteeing you wild jungle sex, but I will fix you a cup of hot chocolate and I promise I won't snore."

"It's a deal," he said. "And in exchange for the hot chocolate, I'll give you the very best back rub of your life."

"Mmm," she moaned softly. "I think I could fall in love with you just for that."

"Good."

Eight

When Libby awoke the next morning, she slipped on a robe—her good cotton eyelet robe as opposed to the ratty flannel one—and wandered out into the office only to discover that David was already dressed and on the phone.

"I'm having breakfast sent over from the Marquis," he said, interrupting his conversation. "I've got the kitchen on the phone right now. Anything special you'd like?"

As someone who was used to deciding between instant oatmeal and cold cereal every morning, Libby thought she'd died and gone to pig heaven.

"Anything?" she asked, just to be sure she wasn't hallucinating or still asleep, dreaming.

David grinned. "Well, anything short of scrambled

ostrich eggs or freshly caught shark steak, I'd say. Just name your pleasure, darlin'."

"Other than you, you mean."

"I'm available," he said.

Now Libby grinned. "Actually, not to disappoint you, but I'm truly starving. Could I have… Let's see. What about a small omelet with hash browns and rye toast? No, wait. Whole-wheat toast with strawberry jam."

He relayed her order into the phone, then asked her, "Bacon or sausages?"

"Bacon." Her mouth was already watering. She hoped she wasn't drooling on the floor.

"Orange juice or pineapple juice?"

"Pineapple," she said, suddenly wondering how long it would take her—once David left town—to get over being so incredibly pampered and rottenly spoiled. Probably forever, she decided.

She walked behind the desk where he sat and bent to kiss the top of his head. He closed his phone, angled his arm around her waist and pulled her closer to him for a moment, burying his face in the folds of her robe.

"I've got a few more calls I need to make, Libby," he said, his breath warm on her hip. "But after that, I'm all yours. We'll do whatever you'd like to do."

"Sounds good to me. I think I'll go take a quick shower before our breakfast comes."

Once in the shower, Libby wondered if it was only yesterday that she'd wept for a solid hour in here while the world, with Haven View at its center, seemed to be falling apart? And then, in a matter of hours, everything had tilted a hundred and eighty degrees and her despair had turned to outright happiness and bright hope for the future. It was like living on a roller coaster.

She shouldn't get too cocky, she told herself. Who knew just what might happen next?

What happened was David got summoned to New York. He'd stayed on the phone while he ate his breakfast, every once in a while throwing her a frustrated glance and mouthing the word *sorry* when he wasn't cursing at whoever was on the other end of the connection.

She honestly didn't mind. It was wonderful to be able to concentrate completely on the best omelet she'd ever had in her entire life. It was as divine as any dessert. She was just chewing the last bit of bacon when David swore once more and stood up, sending the motel's old desk chair rolling backward behind him.

"I've got to leave for New York in—" he consulted his watch "—forty-five damn minutes."

"Oh, David." Libby could feel her mouth turning down at the corners, matching his expression. "On such short notice?"

"It can't be helped. I'm sorry, sweetheart. I'll be back late tonight or early tomorrow morning."

He was already on his way to the door when Libby jumped up to kiss him goodbye in passing.

"I'll be back," he said.

"I'll be here."

Then, in a spray of driveway pebbles and the roar of the Jag, he was gone.

Well, she supposed an architect couldn't do a proper job over the telephone, and it was good that he was so necessary for whatever he'd been summoned for. Libby thought perhaps she'd go to the library today and get some books relating to architecture. It couldn't hurt to be able to discuss it somewhat intelligently with David.

She called Doug then, to see what had transpired last evening during his visit with Aunt Elizabeth.

"I couldn't do it," he said rather mournfully. "We were having such a nice dinner that I just didn't want to spoil it."

"I figured as much," Libby replied.

"What's the rush, honey? Father James's board isn't even going to meet until next week, and I doubt they'll vote on it the very same night. They'll want to think about it for a while. Probably even want to come out and see the place."

She couldn't help but laugh. "You make really good excuses, Doug, for a chicken."

"I admit it."

"Well, you're right, I guess. I don't suppose there's any huge rush, and there's certainly no sense in upsetting Aunt Elizabeth before we absolutely have to."

"Atta girl," he said. "I'm having supper with her again tonight. I'll give her a big hug for you."

After Libby hung up, she glanced outside and saw that her painters had arrived. She was tempted to tell them to take the day off because there would probably be new painters in a week or so, who would be re-painting all the cabins, inside and out, to better learn their craft. Then she decided against it, thinking she might somehow be undermining David's authority, which was the last thing she wanted to do.

With nothing else on her immediate to-do list, she gathered up the breakfast dishes, rinsed them and put them in a box in order to return them to the hotel. Who knew? The chef might be preparing some wonderful experiment for lunch, and she'd arrive just in time to sample it.

Probably not a good idea, she decided, since it wouldn't take long for her to put on twenty or thirty pounds. How in the world could David stay so fit and trim? she wondered. And heaven only knew what Mr. D. E. Halstrom must weigh after indulging for so many years in gourmet meals at his various hotels. The man was probably a blimp.

She left the box of dishes at the front desk of the hotel when no one was looking because she didn't know how to explain why they were in her possession.

After skulking away, she went to the county library, searching through the stacks and the magazine files. It had been a long time since she'd been here, probably since her senior year in high school. She'd forgotten how much she loved this place with its wonderful lighting, the subtle smell of its wooden shelves in the main reading room and the riffling sound of pages turning all around her.

After several hours she learned more about architecture than ever before in her thirty years, from the great Pyramids in Egypt all the way to Louis Sullivan, Frank Lloyd Wright, I. M. Pei and beyond.

Every detail of the occupation fascinated her, not to mention that the research gave her plenty of wonderful ideas for future books of photographs, and a glimpse into David's professional world and a much deeper appreciation of the beautiful glass façade of the Marquis. Libby couldn't wait to discuss it all with him when he returned from New York.

It amazed her, actually, that he seemed so reticent, so truly reluctant to discuss his business. She could hardly say the same about herself, Libby thought. A simple question about cameras or photography in general usually elicited a lengthy, if not too detailed and probably boring, reply from her.

Not so with David. Come to think of it, he had volunteered very little about himself or his profession. Other than telling her he was originally from Texas, which was pretty much a given from his accent, Libby knew almost nothing about him or his family or anything else for that matter.

Well, she thought, slapping closed a heavy coffee-table book on twentieth century midwestern architecture, they were going to have some interesting conversations once he returned from New York. And oh, how she hoped it would be soon because she dreadfully missed him already after just a few hours.

She checked out a few large-print mysteries she thought her aunt Elizabeth might enjoy, then walked out to her car. Much as she hated to admit it, it was a lovely autumn day. With the door open and the late afternoon sun shining on her legs, Libby called the newspaper, punching in the extension for the little darkroom's single phone.

"Is Hannah around?" she asked the man who answered. She didn't recognize his voice.

"Nope. Sorry. She left for the day," he said. "Anything I can help you with?"

"I don't know. Maybe you can. Hannah was going to develop some pictures for me. I was just wondering if she had a chance to do them yet."

"Let me take a look in her secret stash box," he said with a little conspiratorial laugh. "Well, I see two cans of Fuji 400 film here. They yours?"

Libby sighed. "Yes, they're mine. Thanks for your help. I'll give Hannah a call tomorrow."

She'd been hoping the prints would be done and that she could drive downtown, pick them up and then spend a few hours gazing at the furtive long-lens photos she taken of David while he sat on the riverbank in Hannibal.

No such luck.

So Libby returned to the Haven View, where she changed back into her ratty flannel robe and fuzzy slippers and then microwaved some macaroni and cheese. It tasted as horrible as she imagined it would. And the salad she managed to cobble together and douse with bottled dressing wasn't much better.

How could she have become so terribly spoiled in a mere few days? she wondered. This did not bode well at all for her future, whether alone or with a mate.

Maybe when she went back to the library, she thought, she ought to get some cookbooks in order to compete, even minimally, with the gourmet kitchen across the street.

The clunky black telephone on the front desk woke her at eleven o'clock that night. Libby stumbled out of the bedroom to answer it, her immediate thought being that something was wrong with her aunt. When she heard David's voice she didn't know whether to feel enormously relieved or tremendously happy. Both, she decided.

"I miss you," he said. "I had hoped to get back tonight, but that's not happening."

"I miss you, too," Libby said. "How's the Big Apple?"

"Damn lonely without you. I wish you were here."

She couldn't help but smile at that. "Aw, David. I wish I were, too. Hey, you're lucky you're not *here.* I finally had that frozen macaroni and cheese for my dinner this evening, and it was horrid."

"Just call across the street, sweetheart. I'll call the Marquis as soon as we hang up, and tell the kitchen staff to expect it. Order whatever you want, whenever you want it. If you have any problems at all, just call me."

Libby's first instinct was to tell him no because she didn't want to get too terribly used to such a luxury, only to have it disappear when David disappeared. Her actual reply was based more on the thought of, "What kind of idiot would say no to such an offer?"

"Thank you, David," she said. "Although to tell you

the truth, I'd rather have you right this minute than any five-star meal I could imagine."

"I'll be back tomorrow," he said. "Late afternoon, most likely. We'll have dinner and then I plan to make love to you as if the world were going to end in twenty-four hours."

A shiver coursed down her spine. "Is that a threat or a promise?" she asked.

"It's both," he said. "I'll call you just as soon as I get back tomorrow."

Nine

Libby slept in the next morning, something she didn't often do. Since it was Saturday, there were no painters to wake her and the usual morning rattle and clatter of heading-to-work traffic on the highway was merely a low weekend hum.

She thought about calling the Marquis to order breakfast or perhaps brunch. Another omelet sounded so good. She wondered if they had Canadian bacon. Ooh, and melon balls. Libby was practically drooling when she finally decided against it, though. Some-how—she couldn't say exactly why—it seemed to be taking advantage of David's generosity, particularly when he wasn't here to share with her. She knew, when she'd tell him, he'd say that it was foolish, but it was still the way she felt. Had he been with her just then, she'd have ordered double everything.

So, instead of calling the Marquis, she got dressed and drove to her favorite donut shop where she chose a small box of assorted glazed delights to share with Aunt Elizabeth. It was almost impossible not to eat one of them on her way to the rehab facility.

She was glad to see that the crabby roommate wasn't there, but neither was her aunt. Unable to resist the donuts a moment longer, Libby perched on the edge of her aunt's bed and practically inhaled two of them. She was guiltily contemplating a third when the roommate entered, banging her wheelchair against both sides of the door, the dresser and the nightstand before she reached her bed.

"Need some help?" Libby asked as the woman clenched the arms of her wheelchair and began to rise from it.

"Nah. Thanks just the same." She went from chair to bed fairly effortlessly, as if there were nothing terribly wrong with her. "Your aunt's getting her hair done in the little shop downstairs. I don't expect her back for another hour or maybe even more. Those donuts look pretty good."

Libby got up and held the box out for her. "Have one," she said. "They're delicious."

"Thanks. Don't mind if I do."

The woman took three with one quick swoop of her hand, which left one sad little glazed Long John for Aunt Elizabeth. Libby stashed it in the nightstand drawer, then left her aunt a note, saying she'd likely be back tomorrow. With more donuts.

In no huge rush to get home, she took the long way back to Haven View and entered the office just as the phone was ringing. She nearly pole-vaulted over the desk in the hope that the caller would be David. Then, when she heard Doug's voice, she tried her very best not to sound the least bit disappointed.

"Hey, kiddo," he said. "How's my girl?"

"I'm fine," she said.

"I got you a little photo gig, Libby, if you're interested."

As always, this was Doug's way of supplementing her income. If he knew someone who was having a party or some other sort of occasion, he'd convince them that it ought to be memorialized in pictures. Libby usually accepted, more to make Doug happy than to receive the usual few twenties jammed in her hand when she left whatever affair she photographed.

"You'll love this," he said. "They're having a big wingding tomorrow where Elizabeth's staying, and the staff said they'd love some good pictures."

Oh, joy.

"Well, I'd planned to go out there to see her anyway, so I'll just take my camera with me," she said. "What time?"

"It starts at noon, but I don't expect the affair will really get rolling until twelve-thirty or thereabouts."

"Okay. I'll see you there. Or do you want me to pick you up?" she asked.

"Nah. I'm going out there early to help decorate. And, honey, why don't you bring that nice young architect of yours. The more, the merrier."

"He's in New York, Doug. But if he's back tomorrow, I'll ask him. See you there."

Libby hung up, wondering if she had the courage to introduce David to the rest of her wild and wacky geriatric world. At the same time, she wondered about his family, too. Were his parents still alive? Did he have sisters and brothers and a slew of nieces and nephews? Did he have a wonderful dog when he was a little boy? Did he have an ex-wife somewhere? Or children? And, if so, how come he never talked about any of them?

Maybe he just didn't feel comfortable enough with her yet, although she didn't know how that was possible, considering the intimacy they'd shared.

The whole notion of finding out more about his personal life seemed increasingly urgent in light of the fact that he'd probably be leaving St. Louis soon. Then, as she had before, Libby banished that thought from her head. At least as much as she could.

She was going through the mail when she heard a car come to a stop out in front. It wasn't the elegant purr of David's car, but maybe he'd taken a taxi from the airport, she thought, as she went to the office door. No such luck. It wasn't David, and she didn't recognize the man getting out on the driver's side of a white sedan.

"May I help you?" she called. "We're closed right now." She pointed to the sign.

"Sorry. I didn't want to disturb you." He reached into a pocket of his windbreaker and produced a card.

He held it out to her as he walked toward the door. "I'm John Tazwell. I do occasional inspection work for the municipality."

"You're here to inspect the motel?"

"Mostly just to take a look around," he said. "Apparently there have been some complaints about this place."

"Who complained?" she asked sharply.

The man shrugged. "They don't tell me that. They just tell me to go out and have a look at a property. So, here I am."

He was having a look even as he spoke, and to judge from his expression, he wasn't too thrilled with what he saw. She was still miffed that somebody had complained to the local officials rather than to her or to Aunt Elizabeth and Doug. It struck her as extremely rude and underhanded.

"Place looks its age," the inspector said.

Libby couldn't help but laugh. "That's a nice way to say it's fairly downtrodden, I guess. But we're working on that. We really are. It won't be long before everything here looks brand-new."

"New roofs?"

"Yes."

He pointed to the broken lamppost. "Planning to take care of that?"

"Definitely. It's on my list," she said. Actually she ought to bill David for that since he'd frightened her half to death and made her drop the glass.

"You'll need a permit for the roofs." He pointed at all six. "The aldermen voted that in a couple months ago, and most people aren't aware of it."

Libby now counted herself among the clueless. "A permit?"

"It's not complicated, but it needs to be tended to before any work is done, otherwise there's a hefty fine. I know you don't want that. Will there be any plumbing alterations? Showers, tubs, sinks?"

He fired question after question at her, all of which she answered with yes, no or oops.

Finally he closed with, "See that it all gets taken care of. You know, I've always liked this old place. My grandparents stayed here once in the sixties. I can remember visiting them, and using that old swing set." His gaze narrowed as he looked closer at the dilapidated little playground. "Same one, I guess. Imagine that. You're going to replace it, right? I mean, you wouldn't want any little kids to get hurt on that old thing."

By then, Libby could only nod affirmatively. People seemed to be inventing problems and restrictions, simply pulling them out of a hat like big white rabbits in order to torment her at this point.

"Thanks for your time, ma'am. I'll be checking back in about two or three weeks."

Oh, joy, Libby thought.

An hour later she was on her way downtown to pick up her prints from Hannah, who had left a message while Libby was being interrogated by the inspector general. Now how in the world was she going to tell Aunt Elizabeth that the Haven View wasn't up to code in a thousand different ways? She shook her head. Like Scarlett, she'd think about that tomorrow, or maybe even the day after.

As she passed a major shopping mall along the highway, it occurred to her that she really ought to get some new clothes. New man—new clothes. Wasn't there some unwritten rule about that? If not, then there ought to be.

By now, after just a few days and nights, David had pretty much seen her entire wardrobe. Since she hadn't been going out very much in the past year or so, the peach evening dress and various combinations of jeans and tees and sweaters were the sum of it. Maybe she should splurge and get some sexy underwear. Lacy and black. No. Wait. Lacy and red! Would he like that? Probably, she decided, so she planned to stop on her way back home.

Downtown, she parked on the street, fed the meter and then practically raced up the several flights of back stairs to Hannah's dark little domain.

"You're lucky you didn't get here five minutes later," Hannah said. "I was just about to close up and go home."

"Sorry," Libby said, wishing now that she'd used the elevator instead of the stairs. Jeez. She needed to get back in shape.

Hannah made a dismissive signal with her hand. "Don't worry about it. It's not like I have a great date or anything tonight. Truth is I was planning to microwave some popcorn and watch *Gone with the Wind* for the five-hundredth time. Join me, if you want, Libby."

She would have, and quite happily, if she hadn't thought that David would be returning within the next few hours. "Maybe next time, Hannah. I've only seen

Gone with the Wind three hundred times. Clearly, I need to catch up with you."

"Your pictures are over here, Libby. I wasn't snooping or anything, but it was pretty hard not to tell you were in Hannibal. I haven't been there since I was in fourth or fifth grade. Was it fun?"

"It was a blast," Libby said, moving across the little darkroom to the designated shelf. "We really had a great time."

"Who'd you go with? Anybody I know?"

"Oh, just a friend. Not anybody associated with the paper. I'm sure you don't know him."

Libby picked up a few glossy pictures. Tom Sawyer's house, Tom Sawyer's white fence, Tom Sawyer this, Huckleberry Finn that. What she wanted to see was David.

When she reached for the next stack of prints, Hannah said, "Hard to imagine that Halstrom guy in a place like Hannibal, isn't it?"

Libby's hand halted in mid air. "I beg your pardon?" She was sure she hadn't heard correctly. "What did you say?"

"Halstrom. You know. His new hotel is only right across the highway from your place. The great and grandiose Marquis. The mirrored monster." Hannah's arms were crossed and her expression seemed to indicate that Libby might be going deaf or blind, if she wasn't both already.

"I know what it is, Hannah. I just don't know what you're talking about. What does it have to do with Hannibal?"

Libby, of course, knew what it had to do with Hannibal as far as she was concerned. It had to do with David. But there was no way her friend could know that. Was there? She tried hard to recall if Hannah had ever expressed any interest in architecture, but as far as she remembered the woman's only interests were photography and old movies.

Hannah reached out and pulled a photo from the stack. She pointed to the man on the riverbank. "Him," she said.

Libby looked closer. Oh, it was such a good likeness. She'd managed to capture that aura of *I'm in charge here* that so often surrounded him, and there was even a hint, just the slightest, of those adorable smile lines. For a moment, she almost forgot that Hannah was standing next to her, staring at the same photo.

"Him," she said again, stabbing her index finger at the image.

"I see him," Libby responded irritably. "For heaven's sake. I'm the one who took the picture."

"Well, what was he doing in Hannibal?"

Libby rolled her eyes. What a stupid question. "He was sightseeing, of course. What else do visitors do there?"

Hannah snorted. "D. E. Halstrom was sightseeing in Hannibal, Missouri? I mean, it's a neat little place, but it's not exactly on the A list for travelers. What? Has he been to the Eiffel Tower and the Taj Mahal and the Pyramids too many times?"

"I think you're confused," Libby said.

"Well, somebody is." She jabbed her finger again.

"This is the Halstrom hotel guy. The one who's worth billions."

"His name is David."

"Yeah, I know. David Edward Halstrom."

For a second, Libby felt as if she were in a time warp or a science-fiction movie. Everything she knew suddenly seemed to have lost its basis in reality. Her whole head felt like a dark cavern, and her memory seemed like nothing but a blank slate.

Hannah was staring at her. "Hey, are you okay?" she asked. "Do you need to sit down? How about a glass of water? You look like you're about to pass out, Libby."

"That's David Halstrom?" Libby asked. There was a slight tremor in her hand as she pointed to the picture.

"Jeez." Hannah slapped her own forehead. "What have I been saying all this time?"

Libby didn't respond as she gathered up all the photographs and jammed them into her handbag. Finally, she managed to take a deep breath and thank Hannah for developing them.

"I hate to rush," she said then, "but I've really got to get back to the motel. Doug's been there alone all afternoon." It was a lie, of course, but she didn't know what else to say.

"No problem. Hey, I'll walk out with you. Just let me get the lights."

While Hannah busied herself extinguishing bulb after bulb, Libby practically ran for the exit and disappeared down the stairs.

Ten

David looked at his watch for the twentieth time in the past few minutes, and the answer it gave him was the same each time. It's later, you idiot, and she's still not here.

He'd called the Haven View line repeatedly this afternoon on his way back from New York, and each time he listened to unanswered ringing followed by the tape of Libby's slightly-sultry voice saying, "Please leave a message," he'd felt abandoned somehow. Abandoned? It was a ridiculous notion, actually. Almost bizarre. Even when his own father died when David was eighteen and still really a kid, he hadn't felt abandoned. He'd grieved, and then had simply gotten on with what he needed to do.

It barely made sense to him that his usual tightly controlled emotions were suddenly so flimsy and so on edge. Most of the meetings in New York had been dismal and non-productive because he—the boss— wasn't able to fully concentrate on matters at hand. Frankly, he hadn't been able to concentrate at all.

"So, the property is available, David, and highly likely at a relatively good price if we decide to move quickly. I believe speed is of the essence with this one. What do you think?"

"Which property?"

His vice-president in charge of acquisitions swallowed hard and then had tried to disguise a rather long and impatient sigh. "Um. The building on the Upper East Side. The one pictured there up on the screen."

David had blinked at the enormous image of the twenty-story tan brick building right before his eyes, and wondered how long he'd been looking at it without even seeing it. What did he think? Good lord. He wished he knew.

"It depends. What's your ballpark estimate for renovations?" he asked.

The silence in the conference room had been almost palpable then, and he knew those figures had already been thoroughly discussed while he was off in his own little mental wonderland.

Idiot.

So, he'd stood up then, rather brusquely and announced that he had a raging headache. Any decision on this particular project would simply have to wait for further discussion when his schedule permitted. Then he'd stalked out of the room more like a king than the joker he truly was at the moment.

Was this what it felt like to be in love? He shook his head and nearly laughed out loud because it seemed such a juvenile question for a thirty-five-year-old man to be asking himself. He had more than his share of experience in loving, but never before in the falling part of it. Was he falling in love with Libby Jost?

If that was the case, David wasn't sure he cared for it one bit. His temperament, he was fairly sure at his age, wasn't well suited to such emotional ups and downs and that went double where his business ventures were concerned. They'd no doubt lose the Upper East Side property that was the subject of today's meeting because of his damn love-fueled daydreaming and inattention. It was pretty obvious that this "being in love" business could get him in a world of financial trouble faster than he could blink an eye.

On the other hand, he thought, what choice did he have?

He couldn't answer that question at the moment because all he wanted was Libby. Today. Tomorrow. Forever. He sighed. He felt like a fish with a hook firmly implanted in his guts. In his heart, more specifically.

And then he heard the crunch of gravel as her minivan turned into the motel driveway. His internal hook gave a sharp, almost painful little twitch.

White-hot anger, Libby discovered, caused a person to drive much faster than usual. White-hot anger coupled with the knowledge that she'd been horribly deceived caused her to drive even faster, so it wasn't much of a surprise to see the red lights flashing behind her as she traveled west on the highway.

She had pulled over, rolled down her window and handed over her driver's license with barely a peep, fearing that in her current mood she might do or say something that would land her in jail for the next five or six years.

After she took the ticket and resumed her drive home, she thought maybe she shouldn't have been so compliant. Five or six years in jail didn't sound so bad, actually, at that particular moment. In prison, she'd have no motel problems. She'd probably meet some interesting new people in her cell block. She'd lose weight from the not-so-tasty food. And, if given access to her camera and equipment, she could get some great pictures from "inside" and perhaps even put them together in a book.

Best of all, she wouldn't have to see David "The Architect" Halstrom again. Ever.

The instant his identity had registered on her in the newspaper's darkroom, Libby thought she was going to be sick, and she'd done everything she could to get away from Hannah as quickly as her feet would carry her.

How could he have done that to her? *Why* would he have done that to her? She struggled to think of a reason, but couldn't even come close. It just didn't make sense. Why would any man worth what he was worth try to pass himself off as a mere hired hand? He might just as well have told her he was the reservations clerk at the Marquis, or the head chef, or even the elevator inspector.

She didn't like being lied to. She hated it, in fact.

What made it even worse was that he'd lied to her while he was making love to her. Libby didn't know if she could ever forgive that.

How dare he? Her every thought ended with that question. How dare he? And it was what she was thinking when she turned into the Haven View drive. Her heart tripped an extra little beat, and she swallowed hard to still it.

How dare he be here, leaning against his Jag, smiling her way as if everything were fine and dandy? She wanted to step on the accelerator, aim her van in deadly fashion and pin the bastard to his sleek green vehicle. Prison for that? No problem.

Instead she drove the minivan to the rear of the office, where she jammed it into the parking gear, grabbed the keys from the ignition and hoped to scramble into the office's back door and promptly lock it without being accosted by the wretched lizard who was lounging out in front.

No such luck.

She reached to lock the driver's door, but he already had it open a few inches.

"I thought you'd never get home," he said. "I came here straight from the airport."

How could he look so happy? Libby wondered. The man was living a lie while he was acting as innocent as a newborn babe, and—she couldn't help noticing—looking as gorgeous as a cover model. She wondered how many other women he'd deceived.

But what a weird deception, to pass oneself off as relatively poor, at least compared to the man you really were. Was he crazy? Libby felt her eyes widen in fright, and just as the question occurred to her, David took hold of her hand and almost yanked her out of the van.

"I couldn't think about anything or anyone but you, Libby, the whole time I was in New York." His green eyes almost flashed with urgency. "And then when it took you forever to get back here…"

Before he'd even finished his sentence, he was wrapping both his arms around her and drawing her against him. Libby's heart was torn between the hard warmth she'd come to yearn for and the coldness of the lies she'd just discovered. Her hands pushed against his chest even as her head tilted to receive his kiss.

"Libby, oh, Libby," he whispered just as his mouth took possession of hers.

For one long and lovely moment she didn't even have to pretend that she detested this man. She gave herself up completely to the warmth and the wonderfully familiar taste of his kiss. Once again the little electric shocks coursed through her veins and her heart battered against her ribs like a wild bird in a cage. David's arms held her so tightly that she didn't even have to stand on her own. For that long and lovely moment all was right with the world, and Libby wished that she could turn the clock back a few days, even a few hours.

Then hard facts and reality crashed back into her consciousness with a vengeance.

She pulled away from his kiss. "Stop it. Let me go."

David looked at her as if he didn't understand a single word she'd said.

"I said let me go." She flattened her hands against his chest and pushed with all her might.

"Libby, what's wrong?" he asked.

"Let. Me. Go."

He withdrew his arms, and Libby promptly took a step back, at the same time taking a deep breath.

"Now I'd be very grateful if you'd leave, David. Please get off my property."

Once more he looked at her as if her words made no sense to him at all, as if she were speaking Swahili or some ancient, dead language. As if screaming would aid his comprehension, she did just that.

"I said just go. Leave me alone."

Now David took a step back, as if he needed to see her from a different perspective. "I don't understand this at all. Why the hell are you so angry?"

"I don't want to talk about it now." She couldn't talk about it now, she knew, or she'd burst into tears like a fool. She slammed the door of the van, clutched her handbag to her chest and turned toward the office's back door. "Please, just go."

"Libby…"

"Goodbye."

"Libby. Darlin'."

She whirled around to face him. "Don't you *darlin'* me, David Halstrom. Don't you *anything* me ever again. Ever."

Then Libby marched inside, slammed the door in his face and locked it.

In the Marquis underground parking lot, David slammed the door of the Jaguar so hard that its echo was like resounding thunder in the huge concrete cavern. He took the elevator up to the lobby, then strode to the express elevator in order to reach the penthouse, greatly relieved that nobody stopped him for any reason because in his current mood he might have been capable of great bodily harm if not outright cold-blooded murder.

He stared at his reflection in the polished brass interior of the elevator, barely recognizing his own face. There was more than anger in his expression. There was a kind of pain that he'd never seen before. He'd never felt it before, either. And, by God, he never wanted to feel it again.

Once inside the penthouse, he poured himself a stiff drink and took it to the southern window, from which he glared down at the Haven View Motor Court. A part of him devoutly wished he'd never laid eyes on the shabby little place, that the Marquis' penthouse had been designed with a northern exposure, and that he'd never looked toward the south. Not once.

It wasn't true, though. And his heart skipped a significant beat just to remind him. The fact was that he had not only met Libby Jost, but he had fallen head over heels in love with her in what must have been world-record time. David raised his glass toward the shoddy motel.

"Here's to you, Libby, darlin'. Now that you know who I really am, what do you intend to do about it?"

He didn't have a clue how she'd found out, but it had been bound to happen from the second he'd introduced himself to her as an architect. What kind of fool was he, thinking he'd find "regular love" wearing a disguise?

He really couldn't blame Libby one bit for being so angry, as would he if it had happened in reverse. But it wasn't the worst lie that had ever been told. Hell. What if he'd actually been an architect who tried to pass himself off as David Halstrom? Surely that would have been a larger crime and would have angered her even more.

He drained his glass, refilled it, then sat on a leather couch staring south, wondering what to do next. For the first time in his life, David didn't have a clue.

Eleven

The very last thing Libby wanted to do that afternoon was take photographs of the festivities at her aunt Elizabeth's rehab facility. She'd rather do a dozen birthday parties for three-year-olds with amateur clowns, ugly cupcakes and demanding mothers. Actually, she'd rather take a long walk off a short pier.

She'd hardly slept a wink the night before, tossing and turning, getting up for a cup of warm milk, then tossing and turning some more. Finally, at four o'clock in the morning she'd gotten up and put on her ratty blue sweats and running shoes, intending to jog away her problems and anxieties. It didn't work.

Things just got worse when she sat down on a curb and put her head in her hands, intending to work herself up into a good, cleansing cry. Patrol Officer

Tom McKenzie had pulled up in his big white cruiser. He was a really nice guy who made it a point to drive through the Haven View a few times each week.

"Is that you, Libby?" he called out the window.

She lifted her head. "It's me, Tom. Sort of." She gave a wave of her hand. "I'm fine. You don't have to stop."

"You sure?"

No, she wasn't sure at all, but she responded, "Yes. I'm just catching my breath. It's been a long time since I've jogged and I really need to get back in shape. Thanks for stopping, though."

"Well, okay then."

After he drove away, his taillights slowly disappearing down the narrow suburban lane, Libby's wish to drown in tears of self-pity seemed to disappear as well.

The worst part of it was that she couldn't quite decide why she was so angry at David and so wounded by his lie. It made her feel like a fool, actually, to have shared a bed with one of the most successful men in the country, not to mention one of the richest, and not to have known who he was.

She wondered if he did this with all the women he met—introduce himself as somebody else to see if he could get away with it? To have a grand laugh at his victim? Or perhaps, she thought, he did it to avoid being taken advantage of by gold diggers. It made perfect sense in a way, but Libby wasn't yet willing to afford him any motives for his behavior other than perversely criminal ones.

Libby showered and dressed for the big wingding, as Doug called it. Since she'd unofficially be working with her camera, she decided it was fine to dress casually in bleached jeans and a navy turtleneck. Instead of her trusty Nikon and regular film this time, she took her digital SLR which would enable her to send the pictures immediately to the rehab staff.

The party was in full swing when she arrived a few minutes after one o'clock, and Libby put her camera to work immediately in what turned out to be a candid photographer's heaven.

The main assembly room was decorated with silly pumpkins, goofy ghosts made from bedsheets and fanciful scarecrows, all of it topped with twisted strands of autumn-colored crepe paper in red, yellow and brown. The long refreshment table was festooned with real leaves and piles of corn cobs and gourds.

In one corner of the large room was a three-piece band, the musicians—not a one of them under seventy—doing their best to play songs from the 1930s and 1940s for the few brave souls willing to risk further injury on the tiny dance-floor space.

Catty-corner from there, a group of women sat with their knitting and embroidery, little smiles on their faces that seemed to indicate more than a few secrets were shared and gossip exchanged. A bingo game was going full throttle in another corner of the room. Libby managed to get a wonderful shot of a woman's flushed and excited face the exact moment that she yelled "Bingo!"

She was burning film like crazy and really getting into the people and the setting when a warm hand curled around her upper arm and a familiar voice said,

"Your aunt Elizabeth is wondering when you're going to take a picture of her."

Libby almost couldn't breath when she looked up into David's face with its cordial and oh-so-sexy smile. It took a moment for her brain to clear enough for it to register on her that he, of all people, didn't belong here.

"What are you doing here?" she asked him.

"I've been having a cup of hot spiced apple cider and a very nice chat with your aunt Elizabeth," he said. "She's been telling me about your Uncle Joe."

Libby could feel her stomach tie itself into a tight knot. Here we go again, she thought. "He's dead," she said, her tone absolutely flat. "He's been dead for the last six decades."

"I gathered that, Libby," he said softly.

She blinked up at him. "You did?"

"Your friend Doug clued me in, right after I apologized to him for letting him believe I was an architect."

"Oh."

Libby couldn't think of anything else to say. This was all moving way too fast for her. Suddenly it seemed as if David Halstrom, the sleazy liar, was on the inside with her treasured family and she was on the outside staring in.

"I don't want to keep any more secrets from you, Libby," he continued. "The truth is that I came here to talk to your aunt about buying her motel."

"No. You can't," she snapped without even thinking. Well, what was there to think about? "We have plans for it. Well, I have plans. It just isn't for sale."

His voice was low and calm as he replied, "It's not

yours, Libby. As much as you love the place, it still belongs to your aunt. Any decision about selling it is hers, and hers alone."

Argumentative as she felt just then, Libby knew she couldn't argue with that. It was indeed her aunt Elizabeth's place, free and clear. There hadn't even been any debt on the Haven View for the past quarter of a century. In its heyday, the motel had done well enough to pay for itself entirely.

"I know who it belongs to," she said, looking around the big room now. "Where is she? I haven't seen my aunt or Doug yet this afternoon, and I really want to get some pictures of them."

"She's over there." David angled his head toward a set-up of tables and chairs on the far side of the room. "But she sent me over here for one specific purpose. I had to promise, which included crossing my heart and hoping to die and sticking a needle in my eye, that I'd get you out on the dance floor."

Libby lifted her chin and gave a sharp little snort. "Not on your life, Mister."

No sooner were the words out of her mouth, though, than the little three-piece band began playing Glenn Miller's "Moonlight Serenade," one of her favorite songs of all time. When she was a little girl, no more than seven or eight years old, she'd listened to Aunt Elizabeth's old 78 rpm version until she practically wore out the grooves on the brittle old record. Funny. She hadn't thought about that in years, and she wondered if that old record was still around the motel somewhere.

Just then David wrapped his arm around her waist,

and almost before she knew it she was on the little corner dance floor and in his embrace. It was the very last place Libby wanted to be, but there was no denying that it felt wonderful—exquisite!—to be back in his arms, her body pressed tightly against his.

He stood back for a moment in order to gently lift the strap of her camera over her head, then he leaned toward the nearby upright piano, where he set it down, telling the piano player, "Keep an eye on this, will you?"

The old gentleman winked and nodded without even missing a beat in the tune.

David gathered her back in his arms. "Don't fight this," he whispered against her ear. "You'll disappoint your aunt."

Libby snorted again, but this time even she recognized that it was half-hearted and utterly useless. Why, oh, why did his taut, trim body feel so good so close to hers? And why did it set off spectacular Fourth of July fireworks all through her?

"I'm still angry with you," she muttered against his shoulder. "Really angry."

"That's okay." A warm little chuckle sounded just under his breath. "As long as you can be angry and dance at the same time, darlin'."

Apparently she could. Perhaps it was because David turned out to be a divine dancer who communicated every step he wanted her to take by some magic telepathy that went from his hand on her spine directly to her brain and her limbs. They moved on the little dance floor so well, so perfectly in step and in tune, that Libby found herself wishing she were wearing her peach gown rather than her ratty everyday jeans. As long as she felt like Ginger Rogers with Fred Astaire, she dearly wished she looked the part, as well.

She hadn't realized that all the other couples had left the floor to watch them until the music stopped and a spattering of applause coupled with some frail whistles sounded all around them. David graciously acknowledged the cheers, grinning and bowing slightly in their direction. Libby could only blush and hold more tightly to David's hand in the hope that she didn't throw up or pass out as the applause increased and somebody yelled "Encore! Encore!" It didn't take more than a few seconds for an entire chorus to join in.

Dammit. She wasn't meant to be in the spotlight. Her business was behind the lights, taking pictures of those on whom the bright lights shone. Naturally, David was accustomed to all that clamor and adulation, she thought, but she wasn't and she didn't like it one bit. She hated it, in fact.

"So, are you up for one more spin around the dance floor, Libby?" he asked her.

"I'm outta here," Libby announced abruptly.

She wrenched her hand from his, grabbed her camera off the back of the piano and then shouldered her way through the gawkers in the direction of the nearby refreshment table where she hoped that she would find something a bit more bracing there than apple cider.

Just as she was ladling some of the golden liquid into a paper cup, David's voice sounded behind her, but this time there was a slight touch of Bogart in it.

"There's a guy in the kitchen who'll spike that for you for two bucks. Follow me, sweetheart."

Libby had to force herself not to laugh, and as wonderful and medicinal as the kitchen brew sounded to her just then, she declined. Pointing to the camera once more slung from her neck, she said, "Thanks, anyway. I still have a lot of work to do around here this afternoon."

All the merriment seemed to drain from his face in a single instant, and he gazed at her quite soberly. "We need to talk, Libby. Now. Later. Have dinner with me tonight, will you? Let me explain…"

She shook her head adamantly. "I don't think so, David."

Why did he have to be so persistent? It wasn't as if she was the only woman in the world. For heaven's sake, the man probably had a little black book the size of the St. Louis telephone directory with every female listed in it just aching for him to call.

"What are you afraid of?" he challenged her, his green eyes almost penetrating hers with a fierce light.

Libby stiffened. "I'm not afraid of anything."

"Then prove it. Have dinner with me. Please. Give me a chance to explain, Libby. Then, if you still believe I'm lower than the underside of a worm, I'll never bother you again." He raised his right hand. "I promise."

She drained the rest of her cider, then turned back to the table to refill her cup, wondering just how he thought he was going to explain away his deception in any way that she would find acceptable or forgivable. She doubted very much that he could, but admitted to herself that it really wouldn't be fair not to give him the opportunity. For all she knew, he'd probably just dig himself deeper into her enmity.

It wasn't easy pretending that her hand wasn't shaking while she refilled her cup, but her spine was stiff enough and her mind was made up.

Libby turned back to face him. "All right, David. I guess it's only fair to give you a chance to explain. I'll have dinner with you and I'll listen to whatever you think you need to say, but not—absolutely not—in your penthouse at the Marquis."

She didn't bother to add that the memories of that exquisite place and their equally exquisite lovemaking there would haunt her for the rest of her life.

A flicker of relief passed across his expression. "Fair enough," he said. "They've just put the finishing touches on the main dining room, so we'll christen it."

She pictured a great ship getting whacked by a bottle of champagne. With her luck, it was probably the Titanic.

"Eight o'clock?" he asked.

"Eight's fine," she said coolly, already imagining herself back at the Haven View by eleven at the latest and this man already turning into a memory, firmly consigned to her past.

Twelve

After the festivities at the rehab facility, and after Aunt Elizabeth had stubbornly refused to discuss any of her conversation with David Halstrom—other than "Isn't he a nice young man? And so successful! And quite taken with you, Libby, I must say!"—Doug had followed Libby back to the motel, where he made himself comfortable behind the desk and flipped through the latest mail.

Libby didn't really feel like talking. It was four-thirty in the afternoon. She had a headache trying to firmly lodge behind her eyebrows, not to mention a heartache deep in her chest. The mere thought that this evening would be her last with David, even if it was by her very own choice, weighed heavily on her thoughts.

"You know, honey," Doug began as he pulled his

reading glasses down his nose, "This old place served a purpose fifty years ago, in more ways than one, but you've got to admit the old Haven View is way past its prime."

"Yes, I know, but we've got plans to fix that," Libby said. "Father James's board of directors is going to meet in two days, and…"

"And will probably reject the entire idea," Doug said. "They're a pretty conservative group, as I understand, and not inclined to do things that haven't been done before. You need to be aware of that. It was a wonderful idea for this old place, but it might not happen."

"It's such a great opportunity for them," she said.

"They might not see it that way, honey."

He leaned back in his chair now, crossed his arms over his chest and put his feet up on the desk. Libby could tell he had more to say, and somehow she wasn't looking forward to it.

"Your aunt Elizabeth isn't getting any younger, you know, sweetheart," he said. "And, though it might come as a complete surprise to you, neither am I."

Oh, don't, Libby wanted to say. Stop right now, my dearest Doug. I don't want to have this conversation.

"I know that's not easy to hear, honey," he said as if reading her thoughts. "But it's true. It needs to be said."

She felt like a child again, and a somewhat frightened child, too. All she could manage to do was sigh rather loudly.

"Libby, this afternoon David Halstrom presented your aunt with a very sweet offer."

Libby snorted, feeling less like a frightened child now than a betrayed lover. "I'll bet he did."

"This property is worth a pretty penny, you know," Doug continued, "and he offered her all of that and more. In cash. No strung out payments over the years. Just cash. Up front."

Petulantly, she wanted to reply "So?" But she didn't. She just stared across the little office, using her teeth to worry a cuticle on her thumb while waiting for Doug to continue, to drop the other shoe.

"She's considering it," he said.

"Well, that's good, I guess."

His gaze zeroed in on hers. "It is good, honey. I hope she'll have the sense to accept it. And I'm hoping, if she asks for your advice, that you'll encourage her to go ahead with the deal. Or if you can't find it in you to encourage her, then I hope you'll just keep quiet."

Libby wasn't ready to give up all that easily. "But what about all the plans for this place? What about all that money sitting in my bank account, just waiting to go to work around here?"

He rocked back and forth for a moment in the tipped-back chair, then he pressed his fingertips together, and held them almost prayerfully beneath his chin. "If this place is what you want, honey… If this is your heart's desire, then there's no way your aunt will sell it out from under you. All I can tell you is…" He paused for a long, deliberate sigh. "Be very careful what you wish for, Libby, sweetheart. Just be very, very careful."

He didn't give her a chance to respond. Doug heaved forward in the chair, levered himself up and stretched his arms over his head. "Well, this has been a long day, kiddo. I'm going to take myself back to my place for a well-deserved bit of shut-eye."

Libby stood up and met him at the door. She wrapped her arms around him. "Did anybody ever tell you that you're the very best father in the whole world?"

His pressed his lips to the top of her head. "I think somebody just did," he said.

Libby stood in front of the full-length mirror on the closet door a few hours later, making last minute adjustments to the peach-colored dress. She'd already given up on her hair, letting it fall over her shoulders in whatever curls and corkscrews it desired.

She told herself she wasn't dressing for David so much as for the inauguration of the Marquis' dining room, but in the end even she didn't believe that. She was dressing for David, all right. If this was going to be their last evening together, then she damn well wanted him to know what he was losing.

Well, not that he had her to begin with.

Then she heard the crackle of tires on the driveway outside, and mere seconds after that there was a brisk knock on the office door. Ready or not, Libby thought, here we go. After taking a deep breath and one final glance in the mirror, she gathered up her handbag and wrap and headed for the door.

It was Jeff who greeted her. "Good evening, Miss Jost."

Libby stepped through the door and pulled it closed behind her. "Good evening, Jeff."

She couldn't help but wonder if he'd been part of the deception from the very beginning. Still, if he was on David Halstrom's payroll, what choice did the poor guy have? She decided to bite her tongue rather than pepper him with questions that his company loyalty probably wouldn't allow him to answer anyway. She'd simply add that to all the questions she'd stored up for his boss.

He drove the limo out of the pebbled lot of the Haven View, then headed north, across the highway overpass and then turned just a bit west to the entrance of the Marquis, where all the lights were burning bright, as if the place were already full of guests and doing brisk business.

And there stood David, at the front door, looking as if he'd just hired himself to be head doorman. All he lacked was the proper hat, not to mention a patient and helpful attitude.

At the sight of him, Libby wanted to lock the limo doors and order Jeff to step on the gas and get her out of there. Suddenly she didn't want to listen to David Halstrom and his litany of excuses as to why he'd lied to her. She was actually afraid that she might forgive him.

And then what? A few more dazzling nights in his bed and then goodbye? Libby was wishing she'd never met the man when he opened the limo's rear door and extended his hand to her.

She dragged in a deep breath and silently vowed that, no matter what he said, even if it included a deprived childhood, regular beatings and lost puppies and kittens, she would not—absolutely not—forgive him for deceiving her.

* * *

David wasn't accustomed to talking about his private life. He'd been interviewed over the years by the best reporters from all the major newspapers and business magazines, and yet he'd managed to maintain a veil over his life outside of the company.

He wanted to push that veil aside this evening with Libby. He wanted to be honest and forthcoming, to tell her everything about himself from his earliest memories. More than anything else, he wanted her to forgive him.

He'd had the small kitchen crew set up one of the banquettes in the main dining room, so when he saw that Libby had chosen to wear her wonderful peach gown, he was glad he'd chosen the elegant room for their meal.

"This room is gorgeous, David," Libby said as she settled into the banquette.

"Thanks. My design team has been together now for six or seven years, and they've really learned how to put a room together in very little time."

Her head tilted sideways and her lips crooked into an odd little grin. "Am I speaking to David the architect now, or to the real David Halstrom? I'm just curious."

He couldn't help but laugh. "It's funny, you know. There was a time when I was a kid that I really did want to be an architect. I probably had the world's biggest Lego collection. Now I try to have as much input as they'll allow for each one of my hotels."

Now her head tilted the opposite way and David hoped that what he was seeing in her eyes was genuine interest rather than mere politeness.

But, hell, even politeness was a start. At this point, he'd take whatever she was willing to give him and be extremely grateful for it.

Five minutes into their conversation Libby knew she was a goner, and she hated to admit that the sole reason was the tiny little tremor on David's upper lip. If only he'd tried to brazen it out by insisting that the lie he'd told her was small and insignificant, and what difference did it make anyway when all things were considered? Then she would've been able to keep her righteous indignation and her anger stoked for at least another hour or so.

Funny, she thought. The gorgeous décor of the restaurant had no effect on her whatsoever. Sure, there was more crystal dripping from the ceiling than she'd ever seen before in one room in her life and there was enough velvet on the chairs and banquette seats to cover half the city, but she really couldn't focus on anything beyond David's worried face and rather nervous gestures.

"I had the chef prepare the chicken you enjoyed so much the other night," he said when their plates appeared. "I hope you don't mind the repeat performance."

"Mind? I could eat this every night. Thank you."

Okay. So he was thoughtful. She'd give him a few points for that, she decided. He'd even remembered what she had for dinner that night, which most men couldn't do if you bet them a thousand dollars.

When the waiter stood beside their table and expertly uncorked a bottle of wine, then poured a small bit into her host's glass for him to sample, damned if there wasn't a slight tremor in David's hand as he lifted his glass. If Libby was seeking a visible sign of victory, she decided she had it right in front of her, right then and there. Not the outright wail of contrition she wanted perhaps, but it would do.

Of course, that didn't necessarily mean she was going to take up their relationship where it had left off the day before. She had hardly forgotten that her dinner companion was a millionaire many times over, and that he could have his pick of women all over the globe, if not the entire galaxy. Libby had never been known as a shy and retiring little violet, but in this particular case it didn't seem so very odd to wonder, *Why me?*

"You could still be an architect if you wanted to," she said in reference to his earlier statement. "You'd only have to go back to school for a few years."

He sipped his wine, his eyes never leaving hers, then he put down the glass and folded his hands atop the table. "More than just a few years, darlin'. My mother died when I was a baby, and I was barely eighteen when my father died and I had to leave school to take over his business. I had maybe three or four days of college."

"I'm so sorry about your parents, David. I lost both of mine when I was just a baby," she said. "But considering how successful you are, that was obviously all the formal education you needed."

He shook his head. "I've been lucky, to be perfectly honest. More than anything, I've been in the right place at the right time."

The crystals in the dining room fixtures glittered in his eyes as he laughed softly. "But you have to promise not to repeat that, or I'd have to kill you."

Libby sketched a cross over the bodice of her dress. "I promise. My lips are sealed."

"Actually, I've spent the past fifteen years trying to make up for the formal education I missed out on. I've been taking correspondence courses in just about every subject I can find, from anthropology to zoology, and I try to read as much as I can. I've probably enjoyed it more than I would have when I was eighteen. I know I've profited more from it."

Libby was hugely impressed, although she tried not to let it show in her expression. Much as she yearned to find some really horrible, truly hateful qualities in David Halstrom to make it easy for her to reject him, she was becoming more and more impressed with the man. This wasn't at all what she'd planned.

And the more he talked about his past, the more she respected him for not walking away from the family business after his father died, even though it signaled an end to his college days and to his youth. She thought he and her aunt Elizabeth had a lot in common. They were tough hangers on, the both of them. Of course, that still didn't explain or excuse his lie.

When the waiter cleared away their dinner plates and filled their coffee cups, Libby decided it was time to ask since it was obvious by now that he wasn't going to volunteer. As she stirred a teaspoon of sugar into the dark brew, she tilted her head toward David and said, "Did it bother you at all that I truly believed you were the architect who designed this beautiful building?"

He didn't hesitate for a second before he answered. "Yes. It bothered me tremendously. Much more than you can imagine. I regretted the lie the instant it passed my lips."

"Then, why...?"

"Libby, you were my lamppost angel. I didn't want to lose you just a few hours after I'd finally found you. I didn't want to see your sweet mouth making fake smiles and your lovely eyes turn hard and calculating when you discovered who I really was."

In a strange way, it made absolute sense to her. "I take it that happens a lot."

David sighed. "It happens all the time. Like clockwork. And I just couldn't let it happen with you."

She frowned. "That's not much of a compliment to my sterling character, David. You just naturally assumed I was a gold digger like all the others."

"Only because I didn't know you," he protested.

"And now that you do know me?"

"Libby, darlin', if I had to meet you all over again..." He paused to reach for her hand, then held it tightly in both of his as he continued. "I'd get down on my knees and beg my lamppost angel to marry me even before I asked your name."

Her heart did that weird swan dive again. Had she heard him right? Was that some Texas expression she'd never heard before? Or was it—Good Lord!—was it an actual proposal?

How could it be? They hadn't even known each

other a week yet. Then she reminded herself that it had taken her all of about twenty-four hours to fall madly in love with him. Was it possible that the same thing had happened to him? That Cupid had struck them both with a single arrow?

Her hand was still nestled warmly in his as she swallowed hard and decided to ask him exactly what he meant when young Jeff rushed into the quiet dining room. His eyes were huge and full of barely contained panic.

"There's a problem across the highway," he said. "A fire. I've already called 911."

Thirteen

As they raced from the restaurant to the hotel's front door, David used his cell phone to order the limo to the main entrance. It arrived, tires squealing around the corner of the building, only seconds after they had reached the front door.

David ordered the driver out of the vehicle, then jumped into the front seat himself, while Jeff and Libby nearly dove into the backseat. She could already see smoke rising across the highway and a faint but distinct orange glow beneath it.

"Hurry, David. Please," she said.

He hurried. In fact, he pushed the accelerator to the floor and barely braked for the two stop signs between the Marquis and the Haven View. In the backseat, Libby was holding on tight as David swung the big limo into the graveled parking lot and skidded to a stop only feet from the door of the office.

"Oh, my God."

The words left her lips almost like a desperate prayer as she saw the fire leaping from cabin Number Six at the far end of the motel compound. The little cabin was already engulfed in flames.

"Where's the fire department?" Jeff said, the panic obvious in his voice. "I called them. They should be here."

David said nothing. He was out of the limo nearly the second it stopped, looking around as if memorizing the entire situation. "Libby, where's the nearest hose?" he shouted over the roof of the vehicle. "Where?"

Her mind went absolutely blank for a moment. She barely knew where she was herself, only that her whole world seemed to be going up in flames right now.

"Libby," he shouted again. "The hose? A hookup? Tell me where they are."

As she jumped out of the limo, she snapped back to the present and its obvious danger. "Over there." She pointed to the third little cabin. "The hose is hooked up already, I think. It's wound around a holder on the west side wall."

David was running toward the cabin almost before she finished speaking. In the distance now, Libby could hear the high whine of sirens. Why couldn't they get here faster?

She felt paralyzed again, watching the flames eat away at the wood siding of cabin Number Six. There was a slight breeze coming from the west, nudging the flames eastward, toward the next cabin in line. Sparks were already coming down like red rain on the rooftop of Number Five.

Oh, God. Was this how her aunt's lifetime endeavor would end? In flames and ashes? Without her even here for one final chance to see the place, to take it all in as she bid it goodbye? That was a tragedy all by itself.

Then, at last, Libby's professional instincts kicked in. Maybe she didn't know how to put out fires, but she sure as hell knew how to photograph them. She'd been doing it for a decade at the newspaper. She turned to race to the office, where she grabbed her camera, which thankfully had fresh batteries.

If it was all going to end tonight, if this was the last gasp of the Haven View, then Libby would bear witness to its sad and final moments. She aimed her camera and started snapping pictures as soon as she stepped out the office door.

The breeze was blowing harder now out of the west, sending not only bright sparks, but flaming pieces of debris—clapboard and roof tiles—toward the cabin next to it. It wouldn't be long before it caught fire, too.

That's when she caught sight of David. He was standing between the two little buildings, hosing down the adjacent side of Cabin Five and trying to aim water toward its roof. He seemed totally unaware that sparks were landing on him as he attempted to keep the fire from spreading.

"David!" she screamed. She let go of the camera with one hand to wave him toward her. "Get out of there! It's way too dangerous!"

He looked in her direction for a second, but he didn't seem to hear her.

"Get out of there!" she yelled again.

The fire trucks sounded closer now, their flashing lights coloring the view to the east. Hurry, Libby urged them silently. Oh, please, please hurry.

She turned back toward the fiery sight, aiming her camera just in time to capture the collapse of Cabin Six's walls. As they fell in upon themselves, sparks and debris and fierce flames seemed to explode into the night air.

"David!" she screamed again.

Finally, through the black smoke and the falling debris, she saw him drop the hose and race out of the dangerous space between the two cabins, batting at his sleeves and his hair as if he, too, were about to ignite.

Cabin Five's roof went up in flames then just as the big trucks pulled into the drive. The ground shook beneath Libby's feet as the fire engines roared closer. It felt like an earthquake. She took a few shaky steps backward onto the playground gravel and lowered herself to the ground before her trembling legs gave out completely.

From there, she took a few more pictures, but the angle was horrible and because her hands were shaking now, too, she decided to stop being a photographer and simply sit there feeling and no doubt looking like a half-dazed victim.

Jeff came over to sit beside her. She had no idea where he'd been, but in the light cast by the fire she could see that he had soot on his face and his clothes looked damp and rumpled, quite different from his usual well-pressed appearance.

"I'm so sorry about this," he said.

Libby leaned in his direction to gently nudge his shoulder with hers. "Thanks, Jeff. It could've been a lot worse, I guess. At least nobody was hurt."

"Thank God for that," the young man said, his hands propping up his chin as he stared straight ahead at the firemen who were now aiming hoses at the slowly diminishing flames. "You know, just between us, Miss Jost, I didn't think the Haven View was such a horrible place."

He spoke as if the place was already gone, Libby thought. It made her want to weep.

Then he added, "At least I didn't think it was the eyesore that the boss considered it."

"Thanks," she murmured.

So David considered it an eyesore. It shouldn't have surprised her in the least, but Libby still felt betrayed somehow. Her feelings were hurt, as if the old motor court were a close relative whose honor she was obliged to defend. In fact, it was her dear aunt Elizabeth whose honor was involved in this, and Libby would defend her aunt to the ends of the earth, if it came to that.

The thought crossed her mind then that maybe— just maybe—David had arranged for this fire, either through his lap dog, Jeff, or some other underling on his staff. A whispered instruction. Some cash handed over. A few sloshes of accelerant. A match or two. Who would know? And, more important, who would care except Aunt Elizabeth, Doug and Libby?

Maybe his daredevil drive from the Marquis and his

manly and heroic stance with the hose between the two cabins was simply for show. And maybe, just maybe, Libby thought, she was letting her fears and frustrations run away with her.

Then, as she was trying to rein in her worst suspicions, David appeared as if out of nowhere and lowered himself on the ground beside her. The three of them—Jeff, Libby and David—watched in silence as the flames went out, one by one by one.

Half an hour later the air was sodden and acrid. There were no more flames or smoke, but the firemen loitered around Cabins Five and Six just to make certain their work was done.

Libby still sat on the edge of the playground flanked by David and Jeff. Now that there was no longer a canopy of smoke to block the view of the sky, she noticed all the bright stars shining overhead. It struck her as incredibly sad that something so horrible could happen on a night that was otherwise lovely.

Her interrupted dinner in the gorgeous Marquis dining room seemed so long ago she could barely remember it. She did, however, recall David's words and she wondered now if they were merely meant to distract her from what was happening here, across the highway.

She looked to her right. The lights from the fire trucks played across David's face while his gaze was still locked on the devastation on the other side of the driveway. Oh, how she prayed he had nothing to do with the fire. If he did…

A heavily clothed and booted fireman approached them.

"I'm Captain Burford," he said. "I'm looking for the owner of this place."

Libby pushed up from the ground, clutching her peach-colored shawl around her shoulders. "That would be me, I suppose." She extended her hand. "I'm Libby Jost. My aunt is the legal owner, but she's currently in a hospital facility."

"We've got the fire put out for the most part," he said. "It's standard procedure to watch for a while, just to make sure there aren't any flare-ups."

Libby nodded.

"Were you here when it started?" he asked.

She shook her head, wondering if she looked guilty somehow. "No. I wasn't here. I was across the street, across the highway, having dinner." She was about to volunteer David as a witness when the fireman continued.

"Okay. At this point in time, we're relatively certain it was a faulty electrical switch in that last cabin rather than arson. But our inspector will be back in the morning just to have a good look around and to make a final determination."

"Okay," Libby said. So they really were considering arson, she thought. Or maybe they always considered it until they made a final evaluation of a fire.

She cast a quick glance down at David, still sitting on the ground, and didn't see the slightest bit of panic or even concern in his expression. But what did that mean? She already knew the man was a good actor, having convinced her that he was an architect rather than a mega-millionaire.

The fireman was writing something on a clipboard when he said, "I'm going to have to red flag this whole place in the meantime. That means it can't be open for business. Understand?"

"Yes." She nodded again, deciding it would be useless to tell him it hadn't been open for business anyway.

"All right then." He tore off the top copy of whatever form he was filling out and handed it to her. "You don't have to stick around if you don't want to. We've got it under control. But I hope you'll be here tomorrow when the inspector arrives sometime around nine."

Libby took the paper, noticing that her hands had begun to shake once more. "I'll be here," she told the fireman in the same tone she might have responded, "Yes, sir."

She sat back down between the two possible perps.

"All done?" David asked quietly.

"Yes. At least, I think so."

"Then come back to the hotel with me. You don't want to spend the night here, Libby."

No, she didn't. The thought of it alone made her almost panicky.

"Thank you, David," she said.

What choice did she have?

Fourteen

By the time the elevator reached the penthouse, Libby looked half drowned from the spray of the hoses and seemed almost asleep on her feet, so David picked her up and carried her to the beige and pale blue bedroom, the one he'd always considered the most feminine in the suite.

The room had no south-facing window, either. The last thing she needed right now, he decided, was to gaze out at the destruction across the highway.

"Let's get you out of this damp dress, darlin', and then I'll find you something else to wear."

She stood beside the bed like an exhausted child while he unhooked and unzipped the peach dress that now smelled like smoke and ashes instead of lovely perfume. He dipped his head to kiss the cool skin just above her collarbone, and heard a soft little murmur rise up in her throat.

Longing, unlike any he'd ever felt before in his life, ripped through his body like a hot and powerful tide. Nearly overwhelmed by the strength of the emotion, David took a step back and swallowed hard. For a moment he had to force his brain to regroup, not to mention force his bloodstream to remain within bounds.

Good God, how he wanted her. With any other woman, he might have figured "what the hell" and pursued his desire right then and there with little or no regard for her current emotions or delicate state of mind. He wouldn't do that to Libby. He couldn't do it to her. He cared far too deeply for her well-being.

He sighed deeply and turned away to give himself a minute to recover while he went to find something for her to wear. Luckily, there was an ivory silk kimono on a hook in the adjacent bathroom. In the mirror there, David caught a glimpse of himself, the first since he'd left the site of the fire.

Like Libby, he looked as if he'd been through a fiery wringer, too. There were dark streaks of soot on his forehead and cheeks and neck and there were more than a few burnt holes in his shirt. Even the hair on his head appeared to be singed in a couple of places. Once Libby was comfortably asleep, he planned to take a long, hot shower before falling into bed himself.

Back in the bedroom, he found Libby still standing at the side of the bed, staring into space. "Put this on, sweetheart, while I fix you a nightcap."

"Thanks," she said, her voice sounding almost as

listless and worn out as the rest of her. Her eyes glistened but he couldn't tell if she was crying or if it was just irritation from all the smoke.

He picked up the peach dress she'd tossed aside and left in search of some hundred-proof medicine.

In the living room, he poured himself half an inch of brandy, then carried the snifter to the south-facing window. A patrol car was parked in the motel driveway, no doubt stationed there to make sure no flames erupted during what was left of this long night. It seemed odd not seeing the last two little cabins. He almost missed them now that they weren't there.

David thought how the fire would've delighted him last week. Good God, he would've stood here watching, actually cheering on the flames as they coursed through the shabby little place, cabin by cabin. He would've laughed out loud as each wall collapsed, sending fireworks into the night sky. The spectacle would've felt like a victory, another measure of his success.

But that was before Libby. A little smile curved upward at the edges of his mouth. His life now seemed divided into B.L. and A.L. Before Libby and After Libby.

He walked back to refill his snifter and to fix one for Libby. He'd put her dress down over the back of a nearby chair, and his first thought upon seeing it again was to call Jeff to arrange to have the garment cleaned. His second thought was that he would let the poor kid sleep, and maybe even give him a day off tomorrow, or—he looked at his watch—today, actually.

Imagine that, he thought, while he poured several fingers of brandy into Libby's snifter. He seemed to be turning into a nice guy, one who actually cared about other people's feelings. David hoped nobody found out about it. That would definitely be bad for business.

When Libby woke up, she had no idea where she was, but she somehow knew where she was supposed to be at nine o'clock. At the Haven View, with the fire investigator. Unfortunately, the bright blue digital clock on the night table informed her it was way past nine. It was, in fact, just a bit past eleven.

She groaned as she levered up in the bed. She wasn't sure what she was wearing, either, but she knew the silky garment wasn't hers. Good grief. Drawing in a deep breath of frustration, Libby realized that her hair smelled like smoke. Then vivid memories from the night before rekindled in her brain.

There was a quick little knock on the door then. She heard David's voice inquire softly, "Libby?"

"I'm awake," she answered and watched the bedroom door as it opened and David stepped inside.

She was surprised to see him wearing a beautifully fitted gray business suit, complete with matching tie. He appeared fairly well rested, too, which made Libby instantly consider pulling the bedcovers over her head.

"How do you feel this morning?" he asked as he settled on the edge of the mattress.

"Better," she said. "But I'm also feeling rather guilty for sleeping through the meeting with the fire inspector. I wonder if I can call and reschedule it."

"You don't have to. I went as your representative."

"Really?" Libby didn't know whether to be grateful

or suspicious, nor was she sure whether David was helping or hindering. "What did the inspector have to say?"

"Well, first of all, your uncle Doug was there."

She sank back against the pillows. "I should've gotten up this morning to call him and tell him the news. Oh, God. It must've been just awful for him to drive in there and see…"

"It was," David said. "But he's a pretty philosophical guy. He didn't seem to consider it the worst tragedy in the world. Mostly he was just happy and relieved that nobody was hurt."

"Yeah. Me, too," she said softly.

"The inspector will send you a copy of his report, Libby. In a week to ten days, he figured. He spent about an hour going through the place, the burned cabins as well as the other structures. The guy was very thorough."

"And…?" She was holding her breath now, she realized, not that she was expecting David to even mention the word arson, but still…

"And I'd say he's about ninety-nine percent sure that the culprit was the old wiring in the sixth cabin. There wasn't any hint of accelerants or anything remotely suspicious, so the guy ruled out arson right from the beginning. Doug seemed pretty satisfied that his conclusion was correct. He told him that there'd been a fire at one of the cabin outlets a couple of years ago."

"I had no idea," she said.

"Yeah, I know. Doug told me later that they didn't want to worry you."

"Well, we'll just have to update the wiring, I

guess." She tried to sound optimistic. "How difficult could that be?"

David merely shrugged in response. "You aren't going to like hearing this, darlin', but the inspector red-flagged the whole place for the time being."

"What does that mean?"

"Basically, it means zero business activity and zero residence there until another inspection."

Libby moaned as she reached back for a big soft pillow to plop over her head. After a moment or so, she lifted one corner of it in order to look at David and ask, "Is there any other horrible news I need to know about?"

"Nope. That's it for the time being, kiddo," he said, chuckling softly as he reached out to pat her leg. "The good news, though, is that I've got the hot tub going for you, and your breakfast ought to be here in about ten or fifteen minutes."

All things considered, that really did sound like good news to Libby, at least the best she'd heard so far this morning. She'd have plenty of time, she decided, to groan and mope after her body was clean and her stomach was full.

David watched as Libby promptly sank all the way to her adorable chin in the hot tub. If he could've been granted any wish just then, it would've been to repeat this sight, day after day after day, for the next seventy-five years.

He handed her the huge, icy glass of orange juice and then used his thumb to gently erase a little streak of soot on her forehead and another small spot on her cheek.

"No more playing fireman for you, my girl," he said.

"Right back at you," she replied, grinning up at him over the rim of her goblet.

Considering the recent upheaval in her world and that of her loved ones, he was amazed that she could smile at all. After his father had died when he was just eighteen, David couldn't recall smiling for another decade or more.

He'd asked her to marry him the night before, a moment that had caught him completely by surprise. It was as if someone else had been using his mouth to form the words. But right now he knew that he'd meant every word of the proposal. It didn't matter a bit that he'd only known her for five or six days. He should only be so lucky to have this beautiful, brave woman at his side for the rest of his life.

Unfortunately, the object of his unexpected proposal didn't seem to have heard it, or if she had, then didn't seem to remember a single word of it. But, really, who could blame her after the trauma that had followed his question the night before. And right now, David, for all his executive finesse and verbal skills, didn't have the slightest idea how to ask her again.

For all his bravery in business, he felt like a complete coward in his personal life.

"David," she said, her blue eyes widening and gazing up at him through the faint steam of the tub. "Do you, by any chance, know if Doug has said anything to my aunt Elizabeth yet?"

He nodded. "As far as I know, he was planning to visit her this morning and fill her in on everything that happened last night at the Haven View." He knew a bit more than that, but he didn't volunteer it at the moment.

She sighed and sank a few inches deeper into the tub, up to her earlobes now. "She's going to be really upset. Poor thing. That motel is her entire life. And she's going to need a place to stay once they've released her from the center, which could be any day now."

"Well…"

"Well, what?" she asked, cocking her head to the side and narrowing her eyes. "Why am I getting the feeling there's something else you aren't telling me?"

"Well…"

David wasn't accustomed to such back and forth conversations, a bit like the flurry of a table tennis game with nothing getting accomplished. Usually, he said what was on his mind from the get-go. He decided he might as well do that now.

"I offered your aunt a suite here at the Marquis, Libby. For however long she needs it." He looked at his watch. "I expect Doug is telling her about it right now."

She merely stared at him then, for a long, long moment. To David, it seemed like an hour or more under the Spanish Inquisition. He couldn't tell from her expression whether he was about to be thanked or slapped, and he felt baffled enough at the moment not to even know the distinction.

Libby took a long and leisurely drink of her orange juice before she finally deigned to put him out of his misery.

"That was incredibly kind and generous of you," she said. "Thank you, David. Thank you so very much."

He let his breath out slowly, then gestured around himself with both hands. "This is a hotel, Libby. A very large hotel, in fact. There's plenty of room for your aunt and for Doug, too, if and when he decides to join her here."

Water sloshed off her shoulders as she suddenly pushed upward in the marble tub. She set her empty juice glass down on the edge. "Are you kidding me, David? That was one of the options you gave him? Or her?"

"Yes," he said. "Yes, I did." David didn't know why she seemed so startled by this particular offer. "I just assumed they'd been together, the two of them, for a very long time and they wouldn't want to separate now."

Libby was blinking as if she had water in her eyes. "They *have* been together," she said. "But they've never *lived* together. At least not in the three decades I've been around."

It was all he could do not to laugh. "Well, darlin', maybe it's high time they started. I'm sure you know the old expression about it never being too late."

"Hey. I have no problem if they were to live together. I've even suggested it over the years, so it's absolutely fine with me," she said. Then she sighed as she raised her gaze heavenward. "I'm just not too sure about the ghost of Uncle Joe."

"I see what you mean," he said. "I almost believed the guy was alive when your aunt mentioned him to me at the rehab place. She doesn't really believe it, does she?"

Libby shrugged. "Maybe he'll decide to stick around to haunt the Haven View rather than move across the street."

"Well, then. I guess we'll just have to wait and see what happens, won't we?"

Watching Libby sink down once again into the warm water of the tub, David couldn't help but think that "wait and see" wasn't exactly his style. But since he was currently enrolled in Patience 101, he decided he'd just have to…well…wait and see.

Fifteen

Libby barely had time to dry off from her long and relaxing breakfast time in the hot tub when her cell phone signaled for her from somewhere in the depths of her handbag. Still clutching the towel around her, she extracted the phone and answered it.

It was Doug on the other end of the line, practically shouting. "Libby, honey, I've got some great news. The doctors have sprung Elizabeth. We'll be out of here as soon as we can gather up all her clothes and other things."

Libby could feel her mouth fall open as her jaw dropped at least several inches. It was wonderful news, indeed. She just hadn't been expecting it for a few more days. A bit light-headed all of a sudden, perhaps even waterlogged and way too stuffed with scrambled eggs, sausages and toast, she lowered herself onto the edge of the bed.

"But… But where are you planning to take her?" she finally managed to ask.

Doug chuckled. "Well, you know how stubborn she is. I told her about the fire, of course, and then I gave her a choice. I told her it was either my place or the Marquis. And since she's no fool after all these years, and knows all too well that my place is usually a foot deep in dust and half-read books and magazines, she very wisely chose the Marquis."

Libby remembered that David said he'd offered a suite for one or both of them, or all three if Joe's ghost planned to accompany them. For some reason, though, it just hadn't occurred to her that they'd actually be taking advantage of it. And so soon!

"We'll be driving up to the front door of the Marquis just as soon as Elizabeth can get all her junk organized and packed," he said.

It was at this point in the conversation that Libby realized she didn't have anything to wear except the towel that was around her now, or the skimpy little kimono she'd slept in the night before. It was always nice to greet family, especially the elderly, in proper clothes.

"Where are you right now, Libby?" he asked her.

"I'm at the Marquis," she answered. *Virtually naked.*

"Oh, that's perfect. Well, keep an eye out for us, my girl. We should be there…" He sighed. "Eventually."

After she broke the connection, Libby called out to David in the hope of finding her dress from the night before.

"I had it sent to the laundry," he told her. He laughed softly as his warm gaze moved from her chin to her toes. "I wouldn't mind seeing you in only a towel for the next few weeks, I must say."

"Well, I don't think my aunt Elizabeth will say the same, and she'll be here in an hour or so. I need my clothes, David."

As usual, the task fell to Jeff, who was given a list of items to retrieve from the Haven View. He was back in half an hour and Libby was grateful to be wearing something other than a towel, in this case her usual uniform of jeans and a black turtleneck.

While David locked himself away to attend to business, she took the elevator downstairs to wait for her aunt's arrival. Now that the grand opening was just a few days away, it seemed as if the big hotel had suddenly come to life. The lobby was brightly lit and crowded, and there were actual guests checking in. The place truly seemed like a hotel now rather than merely David's private playground.

She walked out the wide front doors into the sunshine to watch taxis and expensive, luxurious private cars come up the long and suddenly busy drive. Whatever had possessed her, Libby wondered now, to imagine that anyone would choose a stay at the Haven View, even a free one, over this magnificent place. If sentimentality had ever clouded anyone's vision, it was certainly true in her case.

There was still a chance, of course, that Father James's board of directors would vote in favor of the old motel as a training center for Heaven's Gate clients, but Libby seriously doubted that the municipal fathers would ever endorse such an operation. Nor would David ever approve of the location of such a facility directly across from the Marquis.

And maybe, after all, he was right.

It was time, she decided, to revamp her plans for that magic fifty thousand dollars. She was starting a mental list of options when she saw Doug's car turn into the Marquis' drive.

Jeff ushered them painlessly through the hotel's registration process, then accompanied them to the beautiful suite on the twentieth floor. There were two lovely bedrooms, two baths, a luxurious sitting room and—wonder of wonders—a small, well-equipped kitchen. It was probably no accident that the windows faced north, and Libby was oh-so-grateful that her aunt didn't have to look out and see the devastation of the motel.

Before he left, Jeff handed Libby the room-service menu.

"They'll bring lunch up as soon as you're all ready to order," he said. "The bill's already been taken care of."

"Thank you, Jeff. For everything," Libby said.

He grinned. "Don't thank me, Ms. Jost. It's all Mr. Halstrom's doing. I just carry out his orders. Besides, it's me who should be thanking you because the boss has been a lot easier to get along with ever since he met you. I hope you'll stick around for a long, long time."

Their lunch arrived in less than half an hour after Libby called in with their order, and the waiter laid it all out beautifully on the table next to the small kitchen. When Libby tried to tip him, the young man refused.

"It's against the boss's orders," he told her. "Enjoy your lunch."

Her aunt Elizabeth, joyous as a kid at the prospect of something other than institutional food, had ordered a fresh-fruit plate as well as a small steak with a baked potato. Libby was astonished to see her practically clean both plates. If she was upset about the fire at the motel, it certainly didn't show in her appetite.

When she had finally finished her meal, Libby refilled her coffee cup and said, "We need to talk about the Haven View, Aunt Elizabeth. Now, if you're ready, but definitely soon."

"Doug and I have already discussed it to death, Libby. Pass me the cream, will you, sweetie?"

Libby looked at Doug then. His neutral expression spoke loud and clear. Don't talk to me. Talk to her, it said.

She tried again. "Well, have you reached any decisions? Or maybe I can help you clarify your options."

Her aunt put down the spoon with which she'd been stirring her coffee. "I don't want you to be upset by this, Libby, but my mind is fairly well made up. I'm going to sell the place just as soon as the paperwork can be put together."

"Sell?" Libby repeated the word as if she didn't understand its meaning.

"Pass me a packet of sugar, sweetie, will you? I thought you might be upset which is why I didn't want to say anything right away, not while we're all enjoying being back together again."

Her aunt ripped open the small packet Libby had put in front of her, and then, just as she was stirring the coffee again, there was a knock on the suite's door.

"I'll get that," Doug said, rising from his chair. "I expect they've come for the empty plates."

Libby sat silently, not wanting to launch into a family discussion in front of a waiter. She was irritated, to put it mildly, that her aunt had seemingly done this sale behind her back. Not that it wasn't her property to keep or sell or burn to the ground if she wanted, but still, Libby felt left out of the process.

"I knew your feelings would be hurt," Aunt Elizabeth whispered as she leaned toward her. "But Doug thought it best if we didn't waste any time under the circumstances."

"What circumstances?" Libby's whisper was more like a hiss, and then she said something she never thought would actually come out of her mouth. "What about Uncle Joe?"

"Oh, honey." Her aunt reached out to pat her hand. "Now I know that you, Libby, of all people, didn't believe a single word of that tall tale of mine."

"But…" No other words were available in Libby's brain just then. She wondered how her aunt could look so composed and calm while her own head was threatening to explode.

"It was just my way of coping, sweetheart," Aunt Elizabeth said almost matter of factly. "And I suppose it was a way of keeping your Uncle Joe alive in some fashion. At least it seemed that way at first."

"But…"

"The more people thought I was nuts, the more they left me alone." Her aunt took a sip of coffee. "Oh, it didn't start out that way. I really did believe my sweet Joe would come home. But after a decade, even I knew he was gone forever. Even so, I kept up my little charade because it helped protect the Haven View. There wasn't a single person at City Hall all those years who'd dare start proceedings against *that poor looney old woman*."

"I wish you'd told me," Libby said when she finally found her voice.

"Well, honey, you were such a smart little girl, and I guess I more or less assumed that you knew since you never asked."

Just then Doug came back with an enormous grin on his face. "Look who's here!" he exclaimed just as David stepped into sight right behind him.

David. In his expensive looking three-piece suit, Italian shoes and an award-winning smile. Everything seemed to fall into place for Libby at the sight of him. The man had been working and plotting and making deals behind her back the whole time he'd been making love to her. She didn't have a doubt in the whole world.

And now the snake passing for a man actually had the nerve to bend down to kiss the top of her elderly aunt's head.

"How's the suite, Elizabeth?" he asked. "There's a larger one available, if this one doesn't give you enough space. All you have to do is whistle, as the saying goes. We can make a change in just two or three hours."

Aunt Elizabeth laughed. "After my previous accommodations, David, this is pure paradise on earth. Please sit down. Join us for coffee, won't you?"

"Thank you," he said.

He pulled out a chair and sat.

Libby couldn't take it one second longer. Her head was about to explode. The moment David's back end hit the chair, she was up on her feet.

"Well," she said, with a perky nod toward her aunt, "I'll check back with you two later. There are a few things I need to tend to this afternoon."

She made a quick retreat, and was nearly to the suite's door when she heard David excuse himself. Once outside the door, she knew there was no way she could get to the elevator before he caught up with her, so she turned toward the nearby fire-escape stairs.

"Libby," he called just as the heavy door was closing behind her.

Damn. Taking the stairs two at a time as if the brand new hotel truly were on fire, she made it down almost two whole flights before David caught up with her.

"Libby." He caught her arm.

Knowing it was useless, she shrieked at him anyway, "Let me go, David."

"Why are you running away from me?"

"I'm not running away. Just let go of me."

"Not until you tell me why. This is crazy, Libby. Why are you doing this?"

"Because, David, you went behind my back and you stole the Haven View from my aunt. Did you think I wouldn't find out?"

He merely stared at her then while he shook his head. "Find out? I assumed you knew. I assumed she told you about our discussions."

"Well, I didn't know. She didn't tell me anything. I just found out a few minutes ago."

Libby was so angry, it was all she could do not to slash out a foot at his shin. "So you gave her…what?…in return for her prime acreage? A midsized hotel suite, some free all-you-can-eat room service and maybe a couple dollars on the side? Was that the deal?"

"Is that what she told you?" he asked.

"No. It's just what I'm guessing a sleazy, conniving real-estate shark would do."

David took a step back, looking at her with a kind of dazed disbelief. "Your aunt hasn't signed the papers yet, Libby, but my offer for the place was three-and-a-half-million dollars, and yes, I did tell Elizabeth and Doug they're welcome to stay here at the hotel however long they like, even if it's years, but that wasn't in any way a part of the deal."

And now it was Libby who took a step back as she blinked up into his face. "Three-and-a-half million? You paid too much, David," she said. "Way too much. That acreage is expensive, but it's only worth two million, tops."

His voice was considerably lower than before and much calmer now, while his green eyes had stopped flashing, having turned back to the deep and sensuous autumn glow that she adored. "Yes, I know exactly what it's worth, darlin'," he said. "Trust me, Libby. It's my business, and I do know that."

"Well, I just don't understand this at all," she said, shaking her head. "I know I'm probably way too protective of my aunt Elizabeth, who doesn't seem to need me even one little bit right now, and at the same time I'm deliriously in love with you, David, and yet I'm so angry with you, I could just…" Her voice sputtered out.

He chuckled. "Well, the love part is good, anyway. We'll have to work on the angry part, though. Come here."

He reached out and drew her into his arms, hard against his body, as he sighed deeply. "I love you, too, Libby, darlin'. I don't know how it happened, or why it happened, but I know I'm yours forever, if you'll have me."

Libby almost laughed as she remembered her confusion about his earlier proposal or non-proposal.

"Just for clarification, David," she said now, pressing her cheek to the warmth of his chest, "would that be a proposal of marriage?"

"Yep. That would indeed be a proposal of marriage. Unless, of course, you'd prefer following in your aunt Elizabeth's footsteps." He stroked her hair. "I just know I want to be with you for the next fifty or sixty years."

"Is that all?"

"Well, it'll do for a start, darlin'."

Sixteen

The next few days seemed to go by in a blur for Libby. She fell asleep in David's arms each night after making delicious love and woke each morning close beside his warm body. But other than those two lovely daily details, there was so much going on at the Marquis that Libby often didn't know whether she was coming or going.

The crowd for the grand opening was enormous, just about filling every suite and room. A two-hour wait for seating in the main restaurant was common. The bar was crowded from the moment it opened each day until it closed for the night. Libby saw more celebrities, both local and Hollywood types, in a few days than she'd seen in the previous thirty years of her life. If she'd been a paparazzi, she would've thought she'd died and gone to celebrity heaven.

"Is it always like this?" she asked David while snuggling close to him in bed.

"Seems like the openings get bigger and more extravagant with each new hotel," he said, a distinct note of weariness in his voice. "But that seems to be what people want these days."

She sighed, angling her face in order to kiss his chin. "I just want you."

"When this is all wrapped up, sweetheart, we'll get away someplace quiet," he told her. "A honeymoon, if you want."

"Oh, that would be lovely."

And it was during those busy, bustling few days that Aunt Elizabeth and Doug's presence at the hotel turned out to be a blessing in disguise. Doug spent a great deal of his time in the lobby, thoroughly enjoying the frenetic activity and people watching and cheerfully volunteering information about local attractions whenever he overheard a guest ask a question.

He was so helpful, in fact, that when David heard about it, he arranged for an information table to be set up in a corner of the lobby, where Doug sat each day, happily fielding questions, making suggestions and handing out tourist brochures. The man had turned into a concierge extraordinaire. Every time Libby caught a glimpse of him, he looked like he was having the time of his life.

Not to be outdone, Aunt Elizabeth—no stranger to the guest business—somehow got hold of a stack of, "How was your visit at the Marquis?" cards, which she thrust into the hands of guests who were checking out or waiting in a restaurant line and insisted they fill out the cards on the spot. She carried extra pens—provided by her sources in housekeeping—in her handbag just for this purpose. "Be honest," she warned them. "Your opinion counts and it means a great deal to us here at the Marquis."

Who was going to deny an eighty-year-old woman on crutches?

Whenever she could get a few minutes of David's time, she went over her notes with him. He was utterly and amazingly patient with her, much to Libby's relief.

"Of course I'm patient," he said in reply to her thanks. "Damned if she isn't finding major flaws in the operation, Libby. There were numerous complaints about the timely delivery of luggage to the rooms during opening week. Aunt Elizabeth's got an idea for color coding the bags from the front desk that will probably cut the delivery time in half. The woman's incredible."

"Well, she's been in this business for a long, long time. You should put her on the payroll," Libby said jokingly. "Doug, too."

"By God, I think I will."

"David! I wasn't serious."

"Well, I am."

Libby really only had one problem left. The magic fifty thousand dollars was still sitting in her savings account, and with the Haven View out of the running as a beneficiary, she needed to come up with another way to use the wonderful gift.

David wasn't much help. "There are countless organizations that could make good use the money, Libby. You don't have to choose just one, you know. You could spread it around."

"That just seems so impersonal," she said, shaking her head. "I'd really like this to be special, David. I'd like it to be much more than merely handing over a check."

It was on the day that she accompanied Aunt Elizabeth and Doug to the lawyer's office to sign the papers for the sale of Haven View that Libby finally found the perfect way to use that magical money.

David had arrived earlier at the law firm to conduct some other business unrelated to the motel's sale. The transaction for Haven View went smoothly enough. Libby hadn't slept well the night before, worrying that her aunt might be overcome with sadness and regret at the last minute and perhaps change her mind.

Rather than sadness, though, Aunt Elizabeth seemed hugely relieved to sign the property and all of its attendant problems over to David. She very nearly glowed when she signed the documents and looked younger than she had in the last ten or so years.

"If that's it," she said, using her cane to rise quite regally from her chair, "I'd like to get back to the Marquis where Doug and I have a great deal of work to do."

There were hugs and hearty handshakes all around, then after they were gone, the attorney leaned back in his chair and asked David if he had any immediate plans for the Haven View property. "I'm inquiring because I have a party who's very interested in that acreage," he said. "Not that he'll match the price you just paid for it, but his funds are ample and he's willing to talk, if you are."

"Well, I…"

Libby interrupted. "David, may I speak to you in private for a moment?"

The attorney, as if he'd heard this exact question or some form of it a thousand times before, immediately excused himself to get some more coffee.

"Don't sell it, David," Libby said the moment he closed the door. "Please, don't sell it."

"Honey, I never intended to. At least not for a long time."

She sighed and sank back in her chair. "Oh, thank heavens."

David reached for her hand and brought it to his lips. "You have a plan, don't you? I can see it glistening in your eyes."

She did, indeed, have a plan.

With a sizeable contribution from David, in addition to her own fifty thousand dollars, the Haven View Children's Park was born.

Libby and her camera spent the next month overseeing every detail of the little wonderland, beginning with the destruction of the poor old worn-out cabins. She kept the lampposts, though. If her aunt wasn't sentimental about the motel, at least Libby felt compelled to keep the lamppost where David had first "accosted" her. Besides, they gave the little park a lovely light after dusk.

It was so lovely, in fact, that Aunt Elizabeth and Doug decided to take their wedding vows there the first week of November, accompanied by a few of their old friends, with Libby and David as maid of honor and best man. It was a beautiful ceremony conducted by Doug's friend, Father James, and when Libby wasn't officiating as maid of honor, she was snapping pictures left and right.

David had offered the newlyweds the company plane and a suite in one of his hotels anywhere in the world for a honeymoon, but they both claimed to be far too busy at the Marquis to take any time off.

"I think we should have our wedding here, too," David said as people drifted away after the ceremony to attend a wedding reception at the Marquis. "This place is truly family."

"Fine with me," Libby said, her teeth chattering as the temperature dropped. She unbuttoned his tuxedo jacket and stepped into his wonderful warmth, planning to stay forever.

* * * * *

"Do I know you?"

"No, Ms. Halliday, you don't. Do I need a note of introduction from my mother?"

Paige felt her cheeks growing hot. "No, no, of course not. It's just…it's just that you don't look like a deliveryman, er, person."

"That's…very comforting, thank you."

Great. Now she was a master of understatement, of the obvious. The guy sure didn't look like a delivery…person. He looked like that perfectly mussed haircut had cost more than the down payment on her condo, his dark suit twice the value of her delivery vans. Tall, slim, handsome, he looked like money should ooze from his pores when lesser people can only sweat.

Still, Paige didn't know the man. "If you could tell me why you're here? I mean, if you're here to talk about decorating your home or business for the holidays, I'm open Monday through Friday. I even have a door on the main street, so you didn't have to come all the way around here into the alley."

"Nobody answered my knock on the front door. And it's after business hours," he said. "But I saw lights on inside, so I thought I'd take a chance. I'm harmless, Ms. Halliday, I promise. In fact, I'm the bearer of good news. And it's raining harder now."

"Oh, all right, all right, come on in," Paige said, backing away from the door. "What's your name, anyway?"

She watched as he went nose-to-nose with a plastic reindeer as he maneuvered his way toward the doorway. "Bru—that is, that reindeer is a real bruiser, isn't he? I'm Sam," he said, clearing the doorway.

Paige had caught the hesitation, the quick recovery. Still, she stuck out her hand. "Nice to meet you, Bru-Sam."

He took it, his grip comfortably firm, his contact just a split-second longer than maybe it should have been. His eyes, now that she was closer to him, were a lovely warm brown. And they were still smiling. "Just Sam, please. I tend to stammer when in the presence of women as beautiful as you, Ms. Halliday."

Paige visibly deflated. "Oh, great. You're selling insurance, aren't you? Look, I'm perfectly happy with the coverage I've got, and I told the guy that when he called last week, okay?"

"I'm not selling insurance, Ms. Halliday," Sam said as he reached into his suit jacket's pocket and withdrew an expensive cream-colored envelope. "I'm here to give you something."

"Sure you are," Paige said, brushing at the silver sparkles on her shoulder yet again. "Why, you're the fifth person this week to stop by in the rain, just to *give* me something." She leaned back against the high worktable, wishing she had worn something classier than black jeans and an old Christmas-green angora sweater to work today.

"Is that so? Lucky you."

She had a feeling she wasn't making a great first impression. Especially since she couldn't seem to *shut up*. "Okay, look, Sam. I'm sorry, I really am. I'm not usually such a grouch. Would you like to go next door to the café for a cup of coffee?" Paige asked brightly. "It can get kind of claustrophobic in here, and Joann's coffee is really good."

And maybe the sexy smell of your cologne will get lost in the other smells and I wouldn't feel so much like jumping your bones.

But she didn't think it would be such a good idea to say that. It wasn't even a good idea to *think* that.

"A cup of coffee sounds very tempting, Ms. Halliday, but I'm afraid I have a dinner engagement in another hour, across town. I'm only here as a favor to a friend. So, if you wouldn't mind, I'd like to just hand you this envelope and be on my way. The letter inside, I understand, is self-explanatory."

"Oh." Paige stared nervously at the envelope, but

didn't attempt to take it from him. "All right. Um… thank you?"

"Not me, Ms. Halliday," he said, and suddenly the man didn't look quite as amused. "Believe me, I have nothing to do with this. Although delighted to meet you, I'm just the messenger."

"You don't look like a delivery guy or a messenger," she told him honestly. Was he flirting with her now? She was pretty sure he was, at least a little bit. Okay. What was good for the goose was good enough for the six geese a-laying, or something like that. She blinked several times, doing her best to look adorably flustered, as they said in the romance novels. "So, no, Sam, I don't think I believed you."

He was staring at her now. Positively *staring* at her. Maybe she looked good in silver spangles? Who knew, it might be a whole new look for her.

"You should believe me, Ms. Halliday, because I'm telling you nothing but the truth. I'm the messenger. My…a client of mine felt he needed someone he could trust to take care of this matter for him. So I may be a messenger, yes, but I'm a very well-paid messenger."

He was looking at her that way again. Why? She wasn't *that* interesting. Was she?

He was so close to her. She could see little reddish flecks in his warm brown pupils. The slight laugh crinkles around the outside of his eyes.

She felt herself almost falling toward him.

Okay, so her body wasn't moving.

Her mind, however, had already jumped into bed with him, and was ripping off his clothes with her mental teeth.

* * * * *

Here is a sneak preview of
A STONE CREEK CHRISTMAS,
the latest in Linda Lael Miller's acclaimed
McKETTRICK *series.*

A lonely horse brought vet Olivia O'Ballivan to
Tanner Quinn's farm, but it's the rancher's love
that might cause her to stay.

A STONE CREEK CHRISTMAS
Available December 2008
from Silhouette Special Edition

Tanner heard the rig roll in around sunset. Smiling, he wandered to the window. Watched as Olivia O'Ballivan climbed out of her Suburban, flung one defiant glance toward the house and started for the barn, the golden retriever trotting along behind her.

Taking his coat and hat down from the peg next to the back door, he put them on and went outside. He was used to being alone, even liked it, but keeping company with Doc O'Ballivan, bristly though she sometimes was, would provide a welcome diversion.

He gave her time to reach the horse Butterpie's stall, then walked into the barn.

The golden retriever came to greet him, all wagging tail and melting brown eyes, and he bent to stroke her soft, sturdy back. "Hey, there, dog," he said.

Sure enough, Olivia was in the stall, brushing Butter-pie down and talking to her in a soft, soothing voice that touched something private inside Tanner and made him want to turn on one heel and beat it back to the house.

He'd be damned if he'd do it, though.

This was *his* ranch, *his* barn. Well-intentioned as she was, *Olivia* was the trespasser here, not him.

"She's still very upset," Olivia told him, without turning to look at him or slowing down with the brush.

Shiloh, always an easy horse to get along with, stood contentedly in his own stall, munching away on the feed Tanner had given him earlier. Butterpie, he noted, hadn't touched her supper as far as he could tell.

"Do you know anything at all about horses, Mr. Quinn?" Olivia asked.

He leaned against the stall door, the way he had the day before, and grinned. He'd practically been raised on horseback; he and Tessa had grown up on their grandmother's farm in the Texas hill country, after their folks divorced and went their separate ways, both of them too busy to bother with a couple of kids. "A few things," he said. "And I mean to call you Olivia, so you might as well return the favor and address me by my first name."

He watched as she took that in, dealt with it, decided on an approach. He'd have to wait and see what that turned out to be, but he didn't mind. It was a pleasure just watching Olivia O'Ballivan grooming a horse.

"All right, *Tanner,*" she said. "This barn is a disgrace. When are you going to have the roof fixed? If it snows again, the hay will get wet and probably mold…"

He chuckled, shifted a little. He'd have a crew out there the following Monday morning to replace the roof and shore up the walls—he'd made the arrangements over a week before—but he felt no particular compunction to explain that. He was enjoying her ire too much; it made her color rise and her hair fly when she turned her head, and the faster breathing made her perfect breasts go up and down in an enticing rhythm. "What makes you so sure I'm a greenhorn?" he asked mildly, still leaning on the gate.

At last she looked straight at him, but she didn't move from Butterpie's side. "Your hat, your boots—that fancy red truck you drive. I'll bet it's customized."

Tanner grinned. Adjusted his hat. "Are you telling me real cowboys don't drive red trucks?"

"There are lots of trucks around here," she said. "Some of them are red, and some of them are new. And *all* of them are splattered with mud or manure or both."

"Maybe I ought to put in a car wash, then," he teased. "Sounds like there's a market for one. Might be a good investment."

She softened, though not significantly, and spared him a cautious half smile, full of questions she probably wouldn't ask. "There's a good car wash in Indian Rock," she informed him. "People go there. It's only forty miles."

"Oh," he said with just a hint of mockery. "*Only* forty miles. Well, then. Guess I'd better dirty up my truck if I want to be taken seriously in these here parts. Scuff up my boots a bit, too, and maybe stomp on my hat a couple of times."

Her cheeks went a fetching shade of pink. "You are twisting what I said," she told him, brushing Butterpie again, her touch gentle but sure. "I meant…"

Tanner envied that little horse. Wished he had a furry hide, so he'd need brushing, too.

"You *meant* that I'm not a real cowboy," he said. "And you could be right. I've spent a lot of time on construction sites over the last few years, or in meetings where a hat and boots wouldn't be appropriate. Instead of digging out my old gear, once I decided to take this job, I just bought new."

"I bet you don't even *have* any old gear," she challenged, but she was smiling, albeit cautiously, as though she might withdraw into a disapproving frown at any second.

He took off his hat, extended it to her. "Here," he teased. "Rub that around in the muck until it suits you."

She laughed, and the sound—well, it caused a powerful and wholly unexpected shift inside him. Scared the hell out of him and, paradoxically, made him yearn to hear it again.

* * * * *

Discover how this rugged rancher's wanderlust is tamed in time for a Merry Christmas, in
A STONE CREEK CHRISTMAS.
In stores December 2008.

Silhouette®

SPECIAL EDITION™

FROM *NEW YORK TIMES* BESTSELLING AUTHOR

LINDA LAEL MILLER

A STONE CREEK CHRISTMAS

Veterinarian Olivia O'Ballivan finds the animals in Stone Creek playing Cupid between her and Tanner Quinn. Even Tanner's daughter, Sophie, is eager to play matchmaker. With everyone conspiring against them and the holiday season fast approaching, Tanner and Olivia may just get everything they want for Christmas after all!

Available December 2008
wherever books are sold.

Silhouette

SPECIAL EDITION™

MISTLETOE AND MIRACLES

by *USA TODAY* bestselling author

MARIE FERRARELLA

Child psychologist Trent Marlowe couldn't believe his eyes when Laurel Greer, the woman he'd loved and lost, came to him for help. Now a widow, with a troubled boy who wouldn't speak, Laurel needed a miracle from Trent…and a brief detour under the mistletoe wouldn't hurt, either.

Available in December wherever books are sold.

Visit Silhouette Books at www.eHarlequin.com   SSE24941

THE ITALIAN'S BRIDE
Commanded—to be his wife!

Used to the finest food, clothes and women, these immensely powerful, incredibly good-looking and undeniably charismatic men have only one last need: a wife!

They've chosen their bride-to-be and they'll have her—willing or not!

Enjoy all our fantastic stories in December:

THE ITALIAN BILLIONAIRE'S SECRET LOVE-CHILD
by CATHY WILLIAMS (Book #33)

SICILIAN MILLIONAIRE, BOUGHT BRIDE
by CATHERINE SPENCER (Book #34)

BEDDED AND WEDDED FOR REVENGE
by MELANIE MILBURNE (Book #35)

THE ITALIAN'S UNWILLING WIFE
by KATHRYN ROSS (Book #36)

REQUEST YOUR FREE BOOKS!

2 FREE NOVELS PLUS 2 FREE GIFTS!

Passionate, Powerful, Provocative!

YES! Please send me 2 FREE Silhouette Desire® novels and my 2 FREE gifts (gifts are worth about $10). After receiving them, if I don't wish to receive any more books, I can return the shipping statement marked "cancel". If I don't cancel, I will receive 6 brand-new novels every month and be billed just $4.05 per book in the U.S. or $4.74 per book in Canada, plus 25¢ shipping and handling per book and applicable taxes, if any*. That's a savings of almost 15% off the cover price! I understand that accepting the 2 free books and gifts places me under no obligation to buy anything. I can always return a shipment and cancel at any time. Even if I never buy another book, the two free books and gifts are mine to keep forever.   225 SDN ERVX 326 SDN ERVM

Name	(PLEASE PRINT)

Address	Apt. #

City	State/Prov.	Zip/Postal Code

Signature (if under 18, a parent or guardian must sign)

Mail to the Silhouette Reader Service:
IN U.S.A.: P.O. Box 1867, Buffalo, NY 14240-1867
IN CANADA: P.O. Box 609, Fort Erie, Ontario L2A 5X3

Not valid to current subscribers of Silhouette Desire books.

Want to try two free books from another line?
Call 1-800-873-8635 or visit www.morefreebooks.com.

* Terms and prices subject to change without notice. N.Y. residents add applicable sales tax. Canadian residents will be charged applicable provincial taxes and GST. Offer not valid in Quebec. This offer is limited to one order per household. All orders subject to approval. Credit or debit balances in a customer's account(s) may be offset by any other outstanding balance owed by or to the customer. Please allow 4 to 6 weeks for delivery. Offer available while quantities last.

Your Privacy: Silhouette Books is committed to protecting your privacy. Our Privacy Policy is available online at www.eHarlequin.com or upon request from the Reader Service. From time to time we make our lists of customers available to reputable third parties who may have a product or service of interest to you. If you would prefer we not share your name and address, please check here. ☐

SDES08R

COMING NEXT MONTH

**#1909 THE BILLIONAIRE IN PENTHOUSE B—
Anna DePalo**
Park Avenue Scandals
Who's the mystery man in Penthouse B? She's determined to
uncover his every secret. *He's* determined to get her under his
covers!

#1910 THE TYCOON'S SECRET—Kasey Michaels
Gifts from a Billionaire
He's kept his identity under wraps and hired her to decorate his
billion-dollar mansion. But when seduction turns serious, will the
truth tear them apart?

#1911 QUADE'S BABIES—Brenda Jackson
The Westmorelands
This sexy Westmoreland gets more than he bargained for when he
discovers he's a daddy—times three! Now he's determined to do
the right thing…if she'll have him….

#1912 THE THROW-AWAY BRIDE—Ann Major
Golden Spurs
A surprise pregnancy and a marriage of convenience brought them
together. Can their newfound love survive the secrets he's been
keeping from her?

**#1913 THE DUKE'S NEW YEAR'S RESOLUTION—
Merline Lovelace**
Holidays Abroad
Initially stunned by her resemblance to his late wife, the Italian
duke is reluctant to invite her to his villa, but it doesn't take long
for him to invite her into his bed.

#1914 PREGNANCY PROPOSAL—Tessa Radley
The Saxon Brides
She's the girl he's always secretly loved—and is his late brother's
fiancée. When he learns she's pregnant, he proposes—having no
idea she's really carrying *his* baby!

SDCNMBPA1108